ANA MARÍA MATUTE

LOS NIÑOS TONTOS | THE FOOLISH CHILDREN
TONTOS |

Translated from Spanish by
María del Carmen Luengo Santaló and **Aileen Dever**

Small Stations Press

CONTENTS

For you

Acknowledgements

We are so very grateful to Carina Pons at the *Agencia Literaria Carmen Balcells, S.A.*, in Barcelona, Spain, for granting us permission to translate *Los niños tontos*. Special appreciation goes to Jonathan Dunne, Director of Small Stations Press, for his personal touch throughout the publishing process, for his prompt emails, for his kindness and his professionalism.

¡Y muchísimas gracias a nuestra familia!

TRANSLATORS' INTRODUCTION

Life

Ana María Matute was born on July 26, 1926 in the beautiful city of Barcelona full of colorful, whimsical designs by architect Antoni Gaudí. She was the second of five children of an upper-middle class family whose father owned an umbrella factory. Because of his business, Ana María Matute poignantly recounted how she and her siblings *"a mitad de curso, cada año, cambiábamos de colegio, de amigos, de ciudad, íbamos de desarraigo en desarraigo. Mis hermanos y yo no pudimos tener amigos. En Barcelona nos llamaban 'los madrileños' y en Madrid 'los catalanes' porque mi familia, a mitad del año, se trasladaba de una ciudad a otra"* (Redondo 60) (in the middle of the school year would change schools, friends, cities, going from one uprooting to the next. My siblings and I could never have friends. In Barcelona we were called "the children from Madrid" and in Madrid we were called "the children from Catalonia" because my family, midway through the year went from one city to the other). Feelings of estrangement from this constant moving back and forth find eloquent expression in her writings consisting of novels, short stories, and children's books translated into over twenty languages (Ortuño Ortín 20). Ana María Matute spent childhood summer vacations and "several long, lonely periods" (Harper 9) recuperating from serious illnesses at her grandparents' home in Mansilla de la Sierra (La Rioja). This mountain village with its "miserably poor people and backward sharecroppers" (Pérez 94) deeply affected the sensitive girl leaving a lasting imprint on her fiction.

9

Only five years old when she began writing and illustrating her own stories, Ana María Matute describes a lively conversation with her father who understood her so well:

Mi padre – fue estupendo en mi infancia, lo que pasa es que lo veía muy poco y hoy ya ha desaparecido – pero me regalaba lápices de colores porque a mí me gustaba pintar y dibujar muchísimo, igual que ahora. Pero luego, "¿Por qué no los quieres más?" "Porque se hacen pequeñitos y luego hay que tirarlos…" "¡Pero no! ¡Ay, si son enanitos!", me decía. Como él me conocía muy bien, era el único que sabía… "Los enanitos a ti te gustan, ¿ves?, la capuchita, la carita". "Oh, sí, ¡claro!" Tenía una cantidad de colecciones, en cajas de cerillas, todo lleno, lleno de enanitos; hasta hacía entierros, pero de broma, porque luego los desenterraba. Hacía unas cosas tremendas de pequeña y yo vivía así. (Nichols 51)

My father – was marvelous in my childhood, the thing was that I used to see him very little and now today he's gone – but he would give me colored pencils because I really loved painting and drawing, just as I do now. But then, "Why don't you want them anymore?" "Because they turn itsy-bitsy and then they have to be thrown out…" "But no! Oh, they're little dwarves!" he used to tell me. As he knew me so well, he was the only one who knew how to reach me… "You like little dwarves, you see? The little hood, the little face." "Oh, yes, of course!" I had lots of collections, in matchboxes, all bursting, bursting with little dwarves; I even used to have burials, but as a joke, because then I'd dig them up. I did some far-out things as a little girl and that's how I used to live.

Ana María Matute's strict and proper mother, though, inspired more fear than affection in her young daughter. The mere sound of her *"tacones lejanos"* (Redondo 16) (distant heels) in the hallway would cause panic-induced stuttering. In a 1989 interview, Ana María Matute said: *"En mis libros, hasta ahora, la madre casi no existe: nunca he querido hablar de una persona que me hizo... sí, voy a decirlo, mucho daño. La indiferencia, el desamor de mi madre, hizo de mí una criatura ansiosa de amor"* (Nichols 39) (In my books, up to now, the mother figure is almost nonexistent. I have never wanted to speak about a person who did me... yes, I'll say it, a lot of harm. The indifference, the lack of love from my mother, made me hunger for love). However, María Paz Ortuño Ortín remarks how Matute's mother *"intuyó el talento y lo diferente que era la pequeña Ana María, guardó todas aquellas libretas en las que escribía sus primeras historias. Se las entregó a Ana María el día de su boda"* (16) (intuited her talent and how different little Ana María was, and kept all those notebooks in which she wrote her first stories. She handed them to Ana María on her wedding day). Regarding her mother, Ana María Matute once commented that with greater perspective *"la fui entendiendo y queriendo, pero durante mi infancia la relación no fue buena... recuerdo que en toda mi vida sólo me dio dos besos... y te los podría describir perfectamente. Los recuerdo con absoluta claridad y emoción"* (Redondo 74) (I came to understand and love her, but during my childhood our relationship was not good... I remember that she only kissed me twice in my whole life... and I could describe those two kisses perfectly. I remember them with complete clarity and emotion).

Ana María Matute's stuttering as a child led to feelings of isolation in school because the French nuns and other schoolmates ridiculed her for it (Redondo 16). Sickly and sad, Matute would often retreat to her magical realms of paper to escape, voraciously reading stories by Hans Christian Andersen, the Brothers Grimm, Lewis Carroll's *Alice's Adventures in Wonderland*, J.M. Barrie's *Peter Pan in Kensington Gardens*, and the tales of Charles Perrault that would so uniquely influence her future writing. Nöel Valis interestingly notes that *"semejanzas entre Matute y Andersen son varias: la visión implícitamente moral; la necesidad y la belleza del sacrificio; la muerte como resolución poetizada; la vida solitaria y patética de los personajes principales"* (Calafell Sala 164) (several similarities between Matute and Andersen include: the implicitly moral perspective; the need and the beauty of sacrifice; death as a poetic resolution; the lonely and pathetic lives of the main characters).[1] Conjuring up fantastic worlds became a way for Ana María Matute to evade some of the grimmer aspects of her childhood (Redondo 14). María Paz Ortuño Ortín considers how Ana María Matute in *"muchos aspectos era una niña rara; era rara hasta para los castigos, la primera vez que la llevaron al cuarto oscuro, encontró en su bolsillo un terrón de azúcar, lo partió en dos y se desprendieron unas chispas en la oscuridad. Había hecho magia. Y su imaginación se disparó; desde entonces, el castigo en el cuarto oscuro era un encuentro con ella misma, imaginaba mundos imposibles, creaba ciudades, bosques, paisajes…"* (17-18) (many ways was a strange girl; she was strange even when it came to punishments. The first time she was taken to the dark room, she found in her pocket a sugar cube which she broke in two and it gave off some sparks in the darkness. She had created magic. And her imagination took off like a shot; from then

---

[1] "The Ugly Girl," the story that opens *The Foolish Children* (1956), reveals a subtle thematic connection to Hans Christian Andersen's "The Ugly Duckling" in the devaluation of a child who does not conform to conventional norms of beauty.

on, the banishment to the dark room was a meeting with her own self, she imagined impossible worlds, she created cities, forests, scenery…).

The Spanish Civil War broke out when Ana María Matute was only ten years old and its impact would leave a deep wound in her soul and psyche. Her father's umbrella factory was seized by the workers and the family found themselves in the Republican zone of Barcelona where they would remain for the duration of the war. From that moment onward, Matute's world changed drastically and she observed: *"Antes vivíamos en una campana de cristal y de repente saltó hecha pedazos"* (Mora 57) (Before we used to live in a crystal bell which suddenly shattered to pieces). Circumscribed to her home during the war years, Ana María Matute escaped through *"una intensa actividad literaria con la que intenta distraer a su familia"* (Redondo 17) (an intense literary activity with which she tries to distract her family), even creating a magazine for her sisters, brothers, and cousins that she entitled *Shybil*.

Ana María Matute donated the stories she wrote as a child to the Mugar Memorial Library of Boston University where the Ana María Matute Collection is currently housed in the Howard Gotlieb Archival Research Center. Exquisitely illustrated by Matute herself, these stories show in embryonic form the brilliance of the future author. Many critics have noted that Ana María Matute's fiction represents an "immediately recognizable blend of lyricism and stark realism, somber intuition and determined sociopolitical *engagement*" (Pérez 93). Throughout her life, Ana María Matute criticized the injustices of the Franco regime and referred to the dictator as *"la momia"* (Schwartz 115) (the mummy). Early on she developed this *"solidaridad con 'los otros', con los silenciados"* (Redondo 17) (solidarity with "the others," with the silenced ones).

When Ana María Matute was asked if she attended university after the war, she replied: *"No me dejaron. Mi formación es autodidacta, aunque creo que me lo he leído casi todo. Tuve suerte al encontrar amigos con vocación de escritores como yo"* (Redondo 61-62) (They didn't let me. I am self-educated, although I believe I have read almost everything. I was fortunate in that I found friends who had literary vocations like I had). During this period in her life, Ana María Matute "discovered forbidden books in the backs of certain bookstores, and so became acquainted with new names and new literary tendencies. She met other young intellectuals interested in literature, restless and rebellious like herself, and began to see them frequently" (Díaz 41). Among this vibrant literary group were Juan Goytisolo, Carlos Barral, and Lorenzo Gomis (Díaz 41).

Though Ana María Matute had never envisioned herself getting married, she became the wife of the writer Ramón Eugenio de Goicoechea in 1952. Janet Díaz reveals how "literary acquaintances of the couple have referred to occasions when journalists or scholars interviewing Ana María Matute were interrupted by her husband who took over the conversation to talk of his own works. It seems that his personality was not one to adapt easily to her greater fame" (52-53). Two years after her marriage, Matute gave birth to her son and only child, Juan Pablo, who became a wonderful inspiration for her writing (Gazarian 182). Unfortunately, the marriage was not a happy one and Ana María Matute initiated a separation from her husband that resulted in the heartwrenching loss of her eight-year-old son who was given into the custody of her husband in accordance with Francoist laws (Redondo 32). About her disastrous first marriage, Ana María Matute has said that *"supuso para mí muchos problemas con mi familia; mi madre me desheredó. Luego fui una de las primeras mujeres de España que se separó legalmente, y sufrí el desgarro de perder a mi hijito durante tres años. Tres años duró el juicio para recuperar su custodia. Mira, se me saltan las lágrimas, no puedo hablar de esta época de mi vida sin llorar, aunque ya han transcurrido más de treinta años"* (Redondo 62) (it created many problems with my family; my mother disinherited me. Then I was one of the first women in Spain to separate legally, and I suffered the anguish of losing my little boy for three years. The trial to win back legal custody lasted three years. Look at me, my eyes are tearing, I can't speak of this time in my life without crying, even though it happened more than thirty years ago).[2] Once she regained custody of her son, Ana María Matute traveled with him throughout Europe and the United States as a visiting lecturer. She became an honorary member of the Hispanic Society of America, *Sigma Delta Pi*, and the American Association of Teachers of Spanish and Portuguese.

Ana María Matute's second marriage to Julio Brocard, *"su gran amor"* (Redondo 32) (her great love), was very happy and lasted 28 years. Feeling personally and professionally fulfilled, she was overcome, however, by a deep depression and consequently wrote almost nothing in the 1970s and 1980s: *"Yo tuve una depresión brutal, espantosa, cuando más feliz era; vivía con el hombre que he querido más en mi vida, con mi hijo al que adoro, no podía irme mejor en el trabajo y en cambio caí en un pozo"* (Redondo 66-67)

---

[2] After her separation from her husband, Ana María Matute expresses her gratitude to her mother-in-law: *"Yo podía no haber visto a mi hijo no ya un solo día, sino nunca. Pero yo tenía una suegra muy buena, que en esto se portó muy bien, y me dijo: 'mira Ana María; tú puedes verlo los sábados'. Y yo lo veía los sábados, me lo llevaba, y así estuvimos dos años y pico"* (Víllora 70) (I could have not been allowed to see my son a single day, or ever. But I had a very good mother-in-law who behaved very well in this matter and said to me: "Look, Ana María, you can see him on Saturdays." And I saw him on Saturdays, I picked him up, and that's how it was for over two years).

(I suffered a brutal, horrendous depression when I was the happiest I'd ever been, living with the man I loved more than any other in my life, with my son whom I adore, things couldn't have been going better for me with my work and yet I hit rock bottom).[3] For those two decades she fell practically silent until her husband's death in 1990, *"el mismo día y hora que había nacido la autora, el 26 de Julio a mediodía, cuando iban a celebrar su cumpleaños. Esta nueva, trágica y simbólica pérdida le obliga a enfrentarse de nuevo con la soledad y con la vida práctica (para la que no parece muy dotada), y sus inexorables necesidades económicas. Después de unos años de desconcierto y dolor la autora comienza, poco a poco, a revisar sus escritos inéditos"* (Redondo 51) (the same day and time the author had been born, the 26th of July at noon, when they were going to celebrate her birthday. This new, tragic and symbolic loss forced her to face loneliness once more and the practical aspects of life (for which she doesn't seem to have been very well suited), and her inexorable financial needs. After a few years of bewilderment and pain the author begins, little by little, to review her unpublished writings).

Some of the numerous literary awards Ana María Matute received over her lifetime include:[4]

Premio Nadal (Nadal Prize) for *Primera memoria* (School of the Sun/Awakening) (1959)
Premio Nacional de Narrativa (National Fiction Prize) for *Los hijos muertos* (The Lost Children) (1959)
Premio Fastenrath (Fastenrath Prize) for *Los soldados*

---

[3] A notable exception to Ana María Matute's literary hiatus was the children's book *Sólo un pie descalzo* (1983) that won a national literary prize.

[4] For a more complete list of Ana María Matute's awards and accolades, visit the following site at the Instituto Cervantes: http://www.cervantes.es/ bibliotecas_documentacion_espanol/creadores/matute_ana_maria.htm.

lloran de noche (Soldiers Cry by Night) (1965)
Premio del Ministerio de Cultura al Libro de interés juvenil (Ministry of Culture Prize to a Book Dedicated to Youth Literature) for *Paulina* (Paulina) (1976)
Premio Nacional de Literatura Infantil y Juvenil (National Prize for Children's and Young Adult Literature) for *Sólo un pie descalzo* (Only a Bare Foot) (1984)
Premio Ojo Crítico Especial (Special Critical Eye Award) for *Olvidado Rey Gudú* (Forgotten King Gudú) (1996)

Ana María Matute also won the National Prize for Spanish Letters (2007) and in 2010, was honored with the Cervantes Prize, the most prestigious literary distinction in the Spanish-speaking world. Moreover, Ana María Matute became only the third woman ever elected to the Royal Spanish Academy and was inducted on January 18, 1998. Various times she was also nominated for the Nobel Prize in Literature (Moix 89). On June 25, 2014, at the age of 88, Ana María Matute died of a heart attack. Sixteen years earlier, in her acceptance speech *"En el bosque"* (In the Forest) before the Royal Spanish Academy, she movingly expressed how *"la palabra es lo más bello que se ha creado, es lo más importante de todo lo que tenemos los seres humanos"* (words are the most beautiful creation, they are the most important of all things we have as human beings).

The Foolish Children

First published in 1956 by Arión (Hernández 297), *The Foolish Children* consists of twenty-one micro-fiction stories about children but not intended for an audience of children. Often referred to as "prose poems" (Díaz 72), the stories vary in length from one unforgettable paragraph as in "The Hunchback" to longer ones like "The Child Who Found a Violin in the Granary." The title *Los niños tontos* has been translated as either *The Foolish Children* or *The Stupid Children* (Díaz 23, 31). Although the word *tonto* (foolish) is not as severe as the English "stupid," what Ana María Matute really means is that these young protagonists are struck dumb by the harshness of the world around them. They are tender souls whose astonishment reminds us of the author herself as a child confronted with the misery of her grandparents' village Mansilla de la Sierra and the violence and death of the Spanish Civil War (Díaz 8). Each delicate story brings to light children who are misunderstood, rejected, and simply unloved. Death is a recurring theme and often implies a solution to the unrelenting cruelty or indifference of the world producing a keen sense of disquietude in the reader. The first story, "The Ugly Girl," appropriately sets the melancholy tone with *"una de las imágenes más comunes de la obra de Matute: una niña aislada"* (Nextext 36) (one of the most common depictions in Matute's works: an isolated child).

Her only work of micro-fiction, Ana María Matute always expressed special affection for this collection: *"No son cuentos, son... ¡niños tontos! No se les puede llamar de otra manera. Yo decía: espera que voy a escribir un niño tonto. Eso mientras estaba en el dentista, en el médico, esperando a Ramón Eugenio en un bar para que me pagara el café. Pero son niños tontos entre comillas, porque precisamente no tienen nada de tontos. Como no se parecen a los otros, la gente decía 'este es tonto'. Pero no lo eran"* (Ortuño Ortín 23-24) (They are not stories, they are... foolish children! You could not refer to them in any other way. I used to say: "Wait, I'm going to write a foolish child." That's what I did while I was at the dentist's office, at the doctor's, waiting in a bar for Ramón Eugenio to pay for my coffee. But they are foolish children in quotes because the last thing they are is foolish. As they were not like the others, people would say: "This one is foolish." But that they were not). Ana María Matute also regarded this slim volume of stories that remains an enduring classic as *"una muestra de mi preocupación por los abusos que se cometen con la infancia"* (Redondo 64) (an example of my concern about how children are mistreated).

Micro-Fiction

There has been a veritable cavalcade of Spanish terms to describe micro-fiction including *"cuentos liliputienses, bonsai, jibarizados, cuentículos, nanoficciones, relatos telefónicos o texticulos, éste con el copyright de Julio Cortázar"* (Ródenas de Moya 77) (Lilliputian stories, bonsai, shrunken stories, little chronicles, teeny tales, telephonic tales or textiles, this last one with the copyright of Julio Cortázar).[5] Micro-fiction stories generally consist of impressionistic sketches of characters and elliptical content from which readers further construct meaning by connecting to their own experiences (Navarro Romero

---

[5] It is interesting to note how the concept of brevity is culture-bound. Micro-fiction stories written in English are generally three times longer than those written in Spanish (Shua 581). As David Lagmanovich affirms, *"lo que en los países anglosajones se considera como un cuento (short story) tiene una extensión – medida en número de páginas o, más técnicamente, en número de palabras – mucho mayor que lo que denominamos de la misma manera en el mundo hispánico"* (22) (what in Anglo-Saxon countries is considered a short story has a length – measured in number of pages or, more technically, in number of words – far greater than what we call a short story in the Hispanic world).

455).[6] Some critics view micro-fiction as a subgenre of the story but for David Lagmanovich it is not *"el producto de un cruce de géneros sino una forma literaria de singular pureza"* (Andrés-Suárez 21) (the product of an intersection of genres but rather a literary form of singular purity). Fernando Valls, specialist in the field of micro-fiction, considers *The Foolish Children* and Max Aub's *Exemplary Crimes* (*Crímenes ejemplares*) pioneer works of the genre (Hernández 299).

Although *The Foolish Children* stands out as significantly different in form and content from what authors were writing in Spain after the Spanish Civil War, Matute probably read examples of micro-fiction. Max Aub's *Exemplary Crimes* was published in Mexico in 1957 but many of his stories had already appeared in his magazine *Waiting Room* (*Sala de espera)* between 1948 and 1950 (Hernández 298). Matute also likely came across short fiction by Juan Ramón Jiménez and Ramón Gómez de la Serna (Hernández 298). Noteworthy among micro-fiction precursors, too, are members of the Generation of 1927, including José María Hinojosa and especially Federico García Lorca whose writing Ana María Matute read and admired at a young age (Díaz 27). One brief narrative by Federico García Lorca is particularly interesting as it is titled "The Hen. A Story for Foolish Children" (*"La gallina. Cuento para niños tontos "*)

---

[6] Micro-fiction stories have existed for quite some time if one considers the brief narratives in the Bible, the tales of Scheherazade, and short narratives intercalated into longer texts (Lagmanovich 17). Ana María Shua comments that with the *"invención de la imprenta, lo primero que se publica después de la Biblia son colecciones de cuentos breves o brevísimos: parábolas, fábulas, cuentos de pícaros, de tontos, enxiemplos y otros vestiglos "* (581) (invention of printing, what's first published after the Bible are collections of short or very short stories: parables, fables, stories about rascals, about fools, exempla, and other such). There was also quite a proliferation of very brief stories in Spanish newspapers beginning in the 1890s (Ródenas de Moya 82-83).

and appeared in the *Semi-Monthly Magazine* (*Revista Quincenal*), Vitoria, in May, 1934 (Hernández 298). The *Foolish Children* became one of Ana María Matute's most notable critical successes and on its publication, Camilo José Cela enthusiastically declared it to be *"una de las más atenazadoras y sintomáticas páginas de nuestra literatura. Los niños tontos marcará un impacto firmísimo en las letras españolas"* (Hernández 311) (one of the most gripping and symptomatic pages of our literature. The *Foolish Children* will leave a very firm impact in Spanish letters).

Shades of Meaning: Color Symbolism
in The Foolish Children

Critic Celia Barrettini observed that the writer Ana María Matute *"no se libera de Ana María Matute, pintora; al contrario, los estudios de pintura van a colaborar en su labor literaria"* (405) (does not free herself of Ana María Matute, the painter; on the contrary, her painting studies will interface with her literary work). Writing at a time of severe censorship as she was (Abellán 19), Ana María Matute carefully selected her palette of colors to portray moods and meanings with the hope, perhaps, that readers would understand her underlying condemnation of Franco's regime through her young protagonists and become inspired to work for change.

From the first line of "The Ugly Girl" the girl's dark skin and eyes are the focus (Matute 7). She can do nothing to erase the stigma of her black skin which is the implied reason the other children reject her. She goes to school well groomed and works hard as *"su cuaderno lleno de letras"* (Matute 7) (her notebook filled with writing) proves. Subtly, the dark-skinned girl becomes interlinked with the apple she eats and the banishment of the biblical Eve. In this case, however, the girl retreats to a garden-like setting. Embraced by the luxuriant colors and beauty of the natural world which provide psychological refuge, she observes the other schoolgirls *"junto a los rosales silvestres, las abejas de oro, las hormigas malignas y la tierra caliente de sol"* (Matute 7) (beside the wild rose bushes, the golden honeybees, the malignant ants and the sun-warmed earth).[7] The golden bees that extract sweet nectar distilled from flowers bring to mind elevation and more luminous levels of consciousness (perhaps faintly foreshadowing the girl's death). The conformity of the ants can be interpreted as a metaphor for the schoolgirls upon whom she also gazes.

One day, Mother Earth tells the girl: *"Tú tienes mi color"* (Matute 7) (You have my same color). In contrast to the insults of the schoolgirls, this voice is soft and soothing. Yet in death, too, the dark-skinned girl is an object to be judged (Matute 7-8). The blue and purple ribbons placed on the girl's wrists bring to mind bruises and handcuffs. In life the girl was enchained by a prejudiced society which was blind to her inner and outer beauty because of its bigoted beliefs. Thus, the girl willingly leaves a sick society that deems her pretty only in death with its imposed values and artificial flowers that are stuffed in her mouth (Matute 8).[8] The darkness of this story has nothing to do with the girl's dusky skin or the tree shadows but with the discrimination she suffers at the hands of children who have implicitly

---

[7] It is as if the protagonist were an audience of one watching a play unfold before her. In several stories there is a theater-like setting as part of the plot which may stem from Matute's early interest in puppetry (Díaz 34).

[8] Janet Díaz explains that the "custom of putting paper flowers in the mouth of a dead child is peculiar to the area of Castile where Matute spent her summers as a child, and is the only textual indication of geographic locale in *The Stupid Children*" (73).

learned from adults how to (mis)treat her. The story ends with the suggestion that after the darkness of the present time (i.e. the Franco regime) a new day will dawn rich in colorful blooms and possibilities.

A compassionate child praises the devil for whom he feels sorry in "The Boy Who Was Friends with the Devil" (Matute 11). For the boy, the devil *"es como los judíos, que todo el mundo les echa de su tierra"* (Matute 11) (is like the Jews, who are driven out from every land). The devil and its traditional red hue may also represent in Matute's story the vanquished Left of the Spanish Civil War. Itzíar López Guil views the devil here as the *"figura de una España vencida, silenciada, en el exilio, y el niño encarna a cuantos, tras la guerra, le mostraban sus simpatías, necesariamente a oscuras"* (343) (embodiment of a conquered Spain, silenced, in exile, and the child represents all those who, after the war, were sympathetic, necessarily in the darkness). Itzíar López Guil also notes that readers of this time period *"no sólo tenían bien presentes a los miles de exiliados políticos españoles, sino también la 'demonización' de los adversarios del nacionalcatolicismo que machaconamente realizaba Franco en sus discursos"* (342-343) (not only had very present in their minds the thousands of Spanish political exiles, but also the "demonizing" of the adversaries of National Catholicism which Franco repeatedly hammered in his speeches). As with Franco's ostentatious manifestations of his religiosity (Romero Salvadó 145), the faith of the boy's mother also appears glaringly superficial; she responds to her son's genuine sympathy by crossing herself and snapping on an electric light (Matute 11). Yet it is the child who sheds light on what true faith means through his thoughtful struggles with the devil (Matute 11). The child's sincerity shines in a society ruled by Franco that is more preoccupied with appearances than authenticity.

Coal dust infiltrates every pore of the young protagonist, even killing birds that are emblems of freedom in "Coal Dust" (Matute 16). As in many of these stories, children are persistently and hierarchically identified with their parents' professions (Hernández 306) and the pervasiveness of the black coal dust further underscores the strict social ranking in Franco's Spain (Romero Salvadó 126). Tragedy strikes when the impoverished girl attempts unsuccessfully to clean off the offending dust that is the stain of her poverty and status (Matute 15). Additionally, the prevailing darkness in which the girl is immersed may symbolize Franco's terrible historical legacy inherited by generations of innocent young Spaniards which cannot be erased no matter how fervent the desire to do so. Yet irresistibly, the girl is drawn to the sparkling water and white glow of the moon. She even marvels how the faucet *"tintineaba, aunque estuviera cerrado, con una perlita tenue"* (Matute 15) (tink-tinked even when off, with a delicate pearl). Dredged from muddy depths, pearls removed from their shells are considered beautiful for their untainted whiteness. The coal dust, however, represents the grimness of the girl's life from which she desperately longs to escape but cannot.

One night the moon comes calling at the window with the hypnotic effect of Lorca's *"Romance de la luna, luna"* (546) (Romance of the Moon, Moon) beckoning to a wider world of opportunities. The silvery moon reflected in the water of the tub symbolizes the illusory quality of life. In these crystalline waters the girl would watch how *"se reflejaban las caras negras de los carboneros"* (Matute 16) (the black faces of the coalmen were reflected). The cleansing water briefly unveils the blackness covering the men's faces that conceals their humanity. Like children in other stories, this girl questions the depressing status quo of her life. The dawn, as it often does, illumines an abrupt, distressing change. In this case, it is the death of the girl and her dreams.

"The Little Blue-Eyed Black Boy" opens with the momentous and auspicious line: *"Una noche nació un niño"* (Matute 19) (One night a child was born). In the full context, the reader knows that the night does not represent potentiality but rather the dimness of this little black boy's future. The use of the diminutive *"negrito"* (little black boy) inspires pathos for this child discarded because of his skin color and considered mentally defective. Yet the reader learns how sensitive, alert, and bright the child truly is. The use of *estar* (to be – state) over *ser* (to be – essence) to describe the boy interestingly treats his skin color as a condition rather than as a natural quality (Matute 19).

Abandoned in a basket, the womb-like shape reinforces the child's rejection and neglect by his mother too. A cat licks the child's face but then *"tuvo envidia y le sacó los ojos"* (Matute 19) (was envious and scratched out his eyes). The eyes were *"azul oscuro, con muchas cintas encarnadas"* (Matute 19) (dark blue, with many red ribbons). The dark blue of the boy's eyes suggests depth and the red a prelude to his suffering. One day the child is lured away by a sweet wind and quietly leaves through a window into the burning sun of a cruel world to *"una hilera de árboles, que olían a verde mojado y dejaban sombra oscura en el suelo"* (Matute 20) (a row of trees, which smelled of wet greenery and cast dark shadows on the ground). The blackness of the tree shadows symbolizes darkness imposed on the green innocence of the child. His blindness leads to synaesthetic descriptions as he yearns for the return of his blue eyes (Matute 20). These sounds and sensations indicate familiarity with the cold as well as the long, distant, lonely train whistle with no one to comfort or care for him.

The boy can be seen as a composite representation of Spain itself with his blue eyes signifying European ancestry and his dark skin the Arab, African, and gypsy. The boy longs to be whole, to unite all of his heritages and identities, which is impossible in Franco's Spain. He patiently sits and waits for his blue eyes, for enlightenment, for change, for compassion, for beauty. Eventually, two gypsies arrive with a large bear and although the gypsies are astonishingly indifferent to the boy's plight, the bear *"se puso a gemir y llorar por él"* (Matute 21) (began to moan and cry for him). The gypsies lash and curse the bear for its pity toward the boy, maybe wishing to reject their own historical legacy of suffering and powerlessness.

The inclusion of the bear *"con la piel agujereada"* (Matute 20) (with a punctured hide) is important. Readers of the time would have been aware that a large, brown bear was the symbol for Madrid that had stood strong against Franco and fascism as this poster published between November 31,1936 and April 21, 1937 represents:[9]

The bear weeps for the blind boy and the darkness imposed on all of Spain by the Franco regime. Though defeated and in chains, the bear's empathetic reaction to

---

[9] Thank you to Lynda Corey Claassen, Director of Mandeville Special Collections Library, UCSD, for the special permission to reproduce this poster here.

the little black boy is striking in this insensitive society. Leaves the colors of the Spanish flag flutter and fall as time passes *"y en lugar de la sombra, bañó al niño tonto el color rojo y dorado"* (Matute 21) (and instead of dark shade, the foolish child was bathed in colors of crimson and gold). The tree trunks *"se hicieron negros y muy hermosos"* (Matute 21) (became black and very beautiful). As in "The Ugly Girl," the color black, at least in nature, is regarded as beautiful. An abandoned dog soon arrives *"color canela que no tenía dueño"* (Matute 21) (cinnamon-colored without an owner) and like the bear, the dog feels sorry for the boy who futilely seeks his blue eyes: *"El perro puso las patas en sus hombros y lamió su cabeza de uvas negras"* (Matute 21) (The dog placed its paws on his shoulders and licked the child's head, a riot of curls like a bunch of black grapes). Again, a new day brings a drastic change with the death of the dark-skinned child. The dog digs a hole to hide the boy; the verb *"escondió"* (Matute 22) (hid) hints at the dog's desire to protect the child who returns to the basket-womb of the earth. The dog's burial of this multi-racial child suggests how Spaniards perhaps with feelings of guilt and shame are concealing and denying their rich, historical and cultural heritage. The blue flowers that blossom in the springtime become a symbol of the redemptive power of nature, of unity, and of hope while the red earth represents the recent wounds the boy and other Spaniards have endured (Matute 22).

The child's precocity in "The Year that Never Came" underscores the repeated theme that these children of Franco's Spain are old beyond their years. Preternaturally aware of the passage of time (Matute 23), this child advances to the door where he sees *"una luz de color distinto a todo"* (Matute 23) (a light with a color that was different from all other things). This light becomes more vivid, expanding, and filling the sky (Matute 23). For balance, perhaps, the child has *"sujeto a cada pie, un saquito de arena dorada"* (Matute 23) (tied to each foot, a little sack of golden sand). The little sacks of golden sand may help maintain stability but this child who wishes to dream is weighed down by the oppressive reality that surrounds him. He hears strident cries from black martins but then the *"grito de los vencejos agujereó la corteza de luz, el color que era distinto a todas las cosas, y aquel año, nuevo, verde, tembloroso, huyó"* (Matute 23) (cries of the black swifts pierced the shell of light, the color that was different from all other things, and that year, new, green, trembling, fled). It is possible that the child is seeing and hearing bombs exploding that create clouds of smoke and a peculiar light that becomes more extensive. The shrieking birds may be the Francoist *vencedores* (victors) piercing the skies with their black bullets and bombs. Yet the little child explains what he perceives through the perspective he has and the new light seems beautiful and different. The color green suggests hope for the young boy's future that is unfulfilled.

Ana María Matute's fascination with color is certainly evident in "The Fire." The child protagonist *"cogió los lápices color naranja, el lápiz largo amarillo y aquél por una punta azul y la otra rojo"* (Matute 25) (grabbed the orange pencil, the long yellow pencil, and the one that was blue-tipped on one end and red on the other) and goes off to mark his own grave. The word *lápiz* (pencil) comes from the Latin *lapis* or stone; a related word is *lápida* (Gómez de Silva 312-313) (gravestone). The use of the preterite in the first two lines indicates the deliberateness of the boy's actions. The two-sided red and blue pencil could be associated with the "reds" of the Spanish Civil War, all the vanquished of various political ideologies who fought on the Republican side, while the blue on the opposite end, the

Falangist militias with their iconic blue shirts (Turnbull 31). The two-colored pencil also signals the essential theme of duality that is repeated with the corner of the house that is half black and half green (Matute 25). In the full context of the story, the two colors are a foreshadowing of the death (black) of the young boy (green) and the potential he represents. Green and black may also imply sickness and rotting (corruption) as a picture of Franco's society.

Due to the repeated whitewashing ritual, *"el niño tenía los ojos irritados de tanto blanco, de tanto sol cortando su mirada con filos de cuchillo"* (Matute 25) (the child's eyes were irritated by all that whiteness, all that sun that cut into his look like the blade of a knife).[10] Part of the boy's anger may come from the white flag of surrender that many Spaniards waved in order to survive during the pernicious Franco years (Romero Salvadó 128). White is also the color of shrouds, of the void, of ghosts, of lives lost. The child feels the rays of the sun like knives cutting into his ability to see. A knife is a tool that acts upon something else as Franco had upon the lives of so many Spaniards. Enraged by the glaring whitewashing done by Franco's regime, the boy *"prendió fuego a la esquina con sus colores"* (Matute 25) (set the corner on fire with all his colors). He has come to understand that the object of the whitewashing is not to reveal, but to dazzle and blind. Matute implies that while some Spaniards were content to accept the gleaming surface of sanctity and rectitude Franco projected, not all were so gullible. For the boy, the brilliant whiteness represents an official façade concealing the dark truths of Franco's Spain as well as his own loneliness. His anger is that of all the innocent children of this era and his fury, quite literally, consumes him (Matute 25).

---

[10] Interestingly, the Falangist anthem was *Cara al sol* (Preston 659) (Facing the Sun).

In "The Washerwoman's Son," the washerwoman emerges as morally superior to the *administrador* (overseer) despite her inferior social status. Diligently she removes the stains, the dirt and grime, created by others. As in "The Ugly Girl," the stone-throwing children have either been taught to be cruel to those considered inferior or allowed to follow natural tendencies without correction. The washerwoman's son is attacked because he is an easy target and his loving mother is powerless to confront the rigid hierarchy that reigns in Franco's Spain. In fact, this boy is doubly inferior in this patriarchal society because of his mother's gender and her menial job. Not unlike Franco himself in his governing style, the *administrador* ostensibly perceives nothing or, more believably, sees all and permits injustices committed directly under his command (Preston 585). Thus the *administrador* does not act to curtail the violence emanating from his own household or to insist on fair treatment for the washerwoman's child whose head is probably scarred from repeated encounters with the bullying stone-throwers. The boy's head is gray, the same color as ancient stones. He is old before his time because of all the negative experiences he has endured. The large size of his head may also imply intelligence and the stones may partly be his punishment for such impertinence given his lack of social status.

His mother plants *"un beso en la monda lironda cabezorra, y allí donde el beso, a pedrada limpia le sacaron sangre los hijos del administrador"* (Matute 30) (a smooch on his hairless head, and in the same spot where she kissed him, he was bloodied by a rock thrown by the overseer's children). The blood and shape of the stones are linked to the mother's mouth and kiss, increasing the pathos of the closing lines. The fact that the attack is premeditated with the bullies waiting behind the blossoming blackberry bushes makes their behavior even more despicable. The flourishing bushes indicate both the indifference and purity of nature in contrast to the nefarious actions of human beings.

The protagonist of "The Tree" believes that through a window he can observe a tree growing on the inside while he is likely actually seeing the reflection on the glass of a tree that is outdoors. Worried about the health of her child and his obsession with the tree, the mother displays her exhaustion in her monotonous repetition, *"No importa, niño"* (Matute 31) (Don't worry, child). As the child dies, he dreams that the tree enters his bedroom and carries him off (Matute 32). Thus during the day, night comes, with no triumph possible over the darkness and hopelessness permeating Francoist Spain (Matute 32). In this story that presents the theme of appearance versus reality, no specific colors are mentioned. Rather, they are implied in words like *"árbol"* (tree – green) and *"noche"* (night – black) (Matute 32) mimicking the idea of reflection. According to Francisco J. Romero Salvadó, with Franco's triumph, children were taught distortions of the truth: "Sycophants and apologists orchestrated official propaganda which had little to do with reality" (128). The child's concentration on the trapped tree inside brings to mind Franco's "Palace of El Pardo" (Preston 345) and the false realities he sought to create as supreme leader.

The doll-like features of the protagonist Zum-Zum in "The Child Who Found a Violin in the Granary" are exquisitely described. He has long, golden hair, eyes that are *"claros y hondos"* (Matute 37) (clear and deep) and lips like *"una pequeña concha rosada y dura"* (Matute 39) (a little seashell, rose-colored and hard). No one has ever heard Zum-Zum speak (Matute 35). In Francoist Spain, many citizens were robbed of their authentic voices and ability to act. Zum-Zum's pink shell of a mouth brings to mind the communists and liberals who were forced into silence. Gilles

Deleuze notes that Zum-Zum's name onomatopoetically imitates the strumming of a violin *"cuya particularidad es ser madera manipulada por el hombre"* (Calafell Sala 167) (whose characteristic is that of wood manipulated by man). Zum-Zum is one among many and the mother in the story appears overwhelmed by her brood. According to Giles Tremlett, such large families "were encouraged by Franco, who saw the number of families with four or more children rise from 116,000 to more than a quarter of a million during his period in power" (213). In addition to criticizing lack of freedom to speak in Franco's Spain, Matute may also be drawing attention to the dictator's promulgation of large families that resulted in a further diminishing of individuality (Matute 36).

In the cornloft Zum-Zum observes how *"se paseaba el sol. Al borde de la ventana vio gotitas de agua, que brillaban y caían, con tintineo que le llenó de tristeza"* (Matute 37) (the sun was glowing. On the edge of the window he saw little droplets of water that shone and fell, with a tinkling that filled him with sadness). Zum-Zum is sad perhaps because the brightness and natural music remind him of possibilities beyond his reach. There is a cage in the cornloft, too, with a *"cuervo negro"* (Matute 37) (black crow) as well as an old dog *"en cuyo lomo había muchos pelos blancos"* (Matute 37) (whose flank was covered with many white hairs). The talking crow in the barred cage represents lucidity trapped by the times. With its jarring voice, the crow speaks the truth and is a symbol of clear-sightedness. Zum-Zum is searching for something in the *"rincones oscuros"* (Matute 37) (dark corners) that turns out to be his voice and the autonomy to become a "real" person. Zum-Zum at last finds a dusty violin with broken strings but the crow declares that a violin is useless if it cannot produce sound but meaningfully uses the personified word "voice": *"De nada sirve el violín, si no tiene voz"* (Matute 38) (The violin is of no use if it has no voice). The crow adds with regard to Zum-Zum: *"Como persona, no sirve para gran cosa"* (Matute 38) (As a person he's not good for much). The dog informs Zum-Zum that the *"violín perdió su voz hace unos años, y tú apareciste en la granja"* (Matute 38) (violin lost its voice years ago, and you appeared on the farm). At the core of this exchange is the superficial harmony that Franco brought to Spain which concealed the cruel and corrupt way he governed (Romero Salvadó 127). The brothers and sisters who gather in the patio want Zum-Zum not only to speak but to sing (Matute 39). Momentously, Zum-Zum hands the violin over to his older brother who says: *"No me mires, niño tonto. Tus ojos me hacen daño"* (Matute 39) (Don't look at me, foolish boy. Your eyes hurt me). Zum-Zum's eyes have the ability to inflict pain because they are his only means of sincere expression. As the older brother plays the violin, he produces *"una música aguda, una música terrible"* (Matute 40) (a shrill music, a terrible music). Suddenly all realize that coming from the violin is Zum-Zum's voice. It is a terrible sound because of the enforced silence he has endured for so long. Zum-Zum then dies in dramatic fashion: *"Todos miraron al niño tonto. Estaba en el centro del patio, con sus pequeños labios duros y rosados, totalmente cerrados. El niño levantó los brazos y cada uno de sus dedos brillaba bajo el pálido sol. Luego se curvó, se dobló de rodillas y cayó al suelo"* (Matute 40) (They all stared at the foolish child. He was in the middle of the patio, with his small lips, rosy and hard, tightly shut. The child raised his hands, and each one of his fingers shone under the pale sun. Then he folded, went to his knees, and collapsed to the ground). The depiction of Zum-Zum holding up his hands to the sun becomes a poignant attempt for him to prove he is a real human being capable of action. But he crumples because without free speech, little action is truly possible. Once Zum-Zum utters a sound, even through intermediaries, any life leaves him. Astounded, the children all rush to Zum-Zum and realize that he was just a doll (Matute 40); the description of his straw-colored hair reinforces his inanimate condition. The ancient, white-haired dog snatches the lifeless Zum-Zum and takes him *"lejos de la música y del tonto baile de la granja"* (Matute 41) (away from the music and the foolish dancing on the farm). The threat of Zum-Zum's voice is gone and the inanity may continue.

Every night the boy leaves the darkness of his poverty to escape in sweet dreams in "The Display Window of the Pastry Shop" (Matute 45). Behind the glass window are mouthwatering apple tartlets, cherries glittering like gems, and pastries glistening with golden caramel sauce (Matute 45). These warm, bright colors are equated with joyful feelings. These are the tantalizing choices available to the moneyed and privileged of Francoist Spain. Others could only stare through glass at what they could not have because of their economic status or party affiliation (which were often cause and effect). The thin, pale dog who faithfully follows the boy increases the pathos and becomes a visible symbol of the boy's pure, animal desire for the pastries. As in other stories, this animal is exceptionally attuned to the boy's feelings.

One night the protagonist becomes particularly consumed by desire with eyes *"barnizados de almíbar"* (Matute 45) (coated with syrup). His eyes have been opened wide to all the delicacies that are beyond his grasp. He leans his forehead on the window, its coldness a reminder of his want. Everything is black inside *"y nada veía"* (Matute 46) (and he could see nothing). The darkness reinforces his bleak circumstances and a child's impossibility of seeing beyond the emptiness of the immediate present (Matute 46).

The child returns home obsessed by his cravings *"con las redondas pupilas, de color de miel y azúcar tostado, muy abiertas"* (Matute 46) (with wide, round eyeballs, the color of honey and burnt sugar). The next morning the boy refuses a ration of chickpeas (whose pale color serves poignantly to contrast the gold of the pastry shop) offered by a charitable woman who leaves scandalized by the impoverished boy's insistence that he is not hungry. He refuses the chickpeas because he wishes to identify with those who eat not out of hunger but for pleasure. Perhaps reminiscing what he has eaten with his eyes, over and over he repeats as in a daze: *"Yo no tengo hambre"* (Matute 46) (I'm not hungry). The superfluous addition of *"Yo"* (I) in Spanish echoes the profound longing to believe his own words and deny that such heavenly indulgences are out of reach for him. The boy's dog goes off in search of a treat for its owner and returns *"trayendo en la boca un trozo de escarcha, que brillaba al sol como un gran caramelo"* (Matute 46) (carrying in its mouth a chunk of ice that shone in the sun like a huge piece of hard candy). In the gloom of his own existence, the boy sucks wistfully on the ice as if it were a piece of succulent, sweet candy that belongs to better times in the past.

The title "The Other Boy" hints at the kind of child the Franco regime was intent on creating: *"Era un niño distinto, que no perdía el cinturón, ni rompía los zapatos, ni llevaba cicatrices en las rodillas, ni se manchaba los dedos de tinta morada"* (Matute 47) (He was a different kind of boy, who didn't lose his belt, who didn't break his shoes, who didn't have scars on his knees or purple ink stains on his fingers). Matute is suggesting that Catholic schools were mass producing stiff, statue-like children without any ostensible moral blemish. Yet she shows how this rigid indoctrination actually resulted in children who were as cold as marble and calmly capable of stealing fruit and torturing dogs (Matute 47). The child in this story *"apareció en la escuela de la señorita Leocadia, sentado en el último pupitre, con su juboncillo de terciopelo malva, bordado en plata"* (Matute 47) (appeared in Miss Leocadia's school, seated at the last desk, with his vest of purple velvet, embroidered in silver). The color purple is not as prevalent as others in nature and contributes to the sense of artificiality. Silver is bright and shining which is how all of Franco's schoolchildren were expected to be. When the teacher discovers *"los dos dedos de la mano derecha unidos, sin poderse despegar, cayó de rodillas, llorando, y dijo: '¡Ay de mí, ay de mí! ¡El niño del altar estaba triste y ha venido a mi escuela!'"* (Matute 48) (the two fingers of his right hand stuck together, which could not be pulled apart, she fell to her knees crying, and said, "Oh my, oh my! The child on the altar was lonely and he has come to my school!") Matute is criticizing the obscurantism of Franco's Catholicism that led to citizens *"sin curiosidad, sin preguntas"* (Matute 47) (without curiosity, without questions).

In the first three lines of "The Girl Who Was Nowhere," the word *"dentro"* (inside) is repeated twice. The reader soon realizes that the *"niña de aquella habitación"* (Matute 52) (girl whose room that was) is there and not there because she has actually grown up to become the old woman with the sallow skin. Images of death and decay abound in the cold whiteness of the winter clothing, reminiscent of a funeral shroud (Matute 51) and perhaps those faded, ash-like flowers in the closet represent a love that never truly blossomed. How carefully the old woman has preserved her treasured memories of youth. Lovingly stored inside the closet is a box that *"guardaba zapatitos rojos, con borla, de una niña"* (Matute 51) (held little red shoes with tassels that had belonged to a little girl). The white clothing is contrasted with these elegant, red little shoes, connoting lost life and vitality. The large-sized doll has big, blue crystal eyes that create a feeling of despairing emptiness (Matute 51). Indifferently they mirror what they "see," unable to register regret over an irrecoverable past. In other times, when the old woman was a child, she would carry that beloved doll to the park and the glass eyes would reflect, as in her child's eyes, a world full of natural beauty and wonder instead of a tomb-like box and closet. The mirror also mimics the blue eyes of the doll with its blank reflections and the old woman's curlers bring to mind the tassels on the little red shoes of long ago.

In several stories, the pleasures of childhood are severely curtailed by economic circumstances. The penurious boy in "The Carousel" briefly makes his dream come true by riding a carousel. The vivid colors of the horses stand for the boy's secret yearning, despite his outward disdain, to join in the fun (Matute 53). Finding a shiny beer-bottle cap, the boy chooses the golden horse with wings and his imagination soars with his longing to rise above his poverty, holding onto one of those *"barras de oro"* (Matute 53) (golden poles). By means of the boy's financial straits, the tarpaulin, and the colorful carousel horses, Matute is showcasing Franco's farcical campaign to rewrite history. Persistently the dictator tried to keep hidden the poverty of so many Spaniards (Preston 594) and he would also unabashedly compare himself to the charging "warrior heroes and empire-builders of Spain's past, particularly El Cid, Charles V, Philip II" (Preston xvii). The child on the golden steed harks back satirically to Spain's glorious past of crusading knights which Franco has grotesquely twisted with his historical *"vueltas y vueltas"* (Matute 53) (spins and spins). The reader is told that the carousel goes round and round *"y la música se puso a dar gritos por entre la gente"* (Matute 54) (and the music began to shriek among the people). The word *"gritos"* (shriek) suggests something out of control which in this case is both the carousel and Franco's brutal regime. In the end, when *"el sol secó la tierra mojada, y el hombre levantó la lona, todo el mundo huyó, gritando"* (Matute 54) (the sun dried the wet earth, and the man lifted the tarpaulin, everybody fled screaming) and light is brought to darkness. The Franco regime deprives children of their childhood and results in death and destruction. Yet Matute implies how one day the cover will be lifted and the ugly truth of the dictator's actions will be exposed for all to see.

In "The Boy Who Didn't Know How to Play," the protagonist scorns brightly-colored toys because they are antithetical to his morose personality (Matute 57). The toys appear shrill to him as they are not in harmony with his negative impulses. The reference to the roundness of the ball and the wheels on the little truck insinuate a balance that this child lacks. His paleness is an indication of his bloodthirstiness and the reader learns how those hands that dangle limply can be moved to kill. The mother *"miraba inquieta al niño, que iba y venía con una sombra entre los ojos"* (Matute 57) (anxiously watched the boy come and go with a shadow between her eyes). The word *"sombra"* (shadow) signals her worry and niggling fear that there is something psychologically wrong with her son. One day she follows him unobserved with the rain darkening the pessimistic mood and its implied discomfort showing how determined she is to discover what is going on with her child (Matute 58). The little creatures the boy captures and kills are devoid of bright coloration like his own personal world (Matute 58). Watching her son sever these creatures' heads, the mother must feel deep sadness and something akin to despair. One of the signs of a future serial killer, as we know today, is the abuse of animals as a child (Vronsky 77). The boy does not merely step on the creatures but causes their deaths up close. The dirtiness of his nails points to a moral darkness just beneath the surface. In a wider context, Matute is saying that the children of Franco's Spain do not know how to play but they know how to suffer and kill.

The moneylender's son in "The Little Paschal Lamb" is an object of mockery due to his weight but also because of his father's greed and insensitivity (Matute 59). As a gift, the child is given *"un corderito pascual"* (Matute 59) (a little paschal lamb). The adjective *"pascual"* (paschal) means Easter but it is also a masculine name that was common in Spain and humanizes the little lamb even further. The use of the diminutive *"corderito"* (little lamb) additionally contributes to the poignancy of the story. This little lamb *"era blanco y dulce, y le pusieron un lazo verde al cuello"* (Matute 59) (was white and sweet, and they put a green ribbon around its neck). The green ribbon represents the bond of simple, innocent friendship shared between the young boy and lamb that is as sweet as the green grass the boy seeks for his pet (Matute 59). The lamb's whiteness points also to the purity of their bond; this child has no friends but the little lamb accepts him just the way he is (Matute 59). The creature's soft, nonjudgmental eyes are a source of relief to the boy whose kind treatment of the lamb is juxtaposed with his father's unremitting callousness. When spring arrives and children are taken to the uncompromising moneylender, the *"abriguitos y los pantalones de lana se amontonaban en las estanterías"* (Matute 60) (little coats and the woolen pants were heaped onto the shelves). With the mention of *"lana"* (woolen), the reader understands how these children, too, are little lambs in a harsh world.

At Easter, *"cuando el niño del ropavejero se sentó a la mesa llena de cuchillos y de sol sobre el mantel, vio de pronto los dientes de papá, los grandes y blancos dientes"* (Matute 61) (when the old clothes dealer's child sat at the table full of knives and sunshine beaming on the tablecloth, he suddenly saw *papá's* teeth, the big and white teeth). The theater-like setting with the bright tablecloth and shiny silverware deepens the sinister scene. The knives echo the father's large, white teeth and animalistic nature while the sunlight symbolizes illumination as the boy abruptly leaps up with a horrifying suspicion and runs into the kitchen (Matute 61). The lamb, and the boy, too, are sacrificial victims. The boy's innocence has been given up to satisfy his father's gluttony. Not unlike this cruel father, Franco possessed astonishing sang-froid (Preston 227).

"The Child of the Hunter" depicts a child following the actions of his father and role model (Matute 65). Returning at night with pigeons and rabbits dangling from their belts, their legs would become bespattered with *"gotitas rojas, que, poco a poco, se volvían negras"* (Matute 65) (little red droplets which, little by little, turned black). The red drops of blood that turn black foreshadow how the boy will hunt the stars dotting the sky. One night when there is a full moon, the boy steals his father's shotgun and goes up into the forested mountain. The image of traipsing *"camino arriba"* (Matute 65) (up hill) shows how hunting is the height of achievement in this boy's mind. Once there, the boy *"cazó todas las estrellas de la noche, las alondras blancas, las liebres azules, las palomas verdes, las hojas dorados y el viento puntiagudo. Cazó el miedo, el frío, la oscuridad"* (Matute 66) (hunted all the stars of the night, the white larks, the blue hares, the green pigeons, the golden leaves and the sharp wind. He hunted fear, cold, darkness). The explosion of colors represents the boy's overcharged imagination and aspirations. Reality and fantasy have become interfused yet the author's underlying message is that Franco, an avid hunter himself (Preston 640), has created a nation of insensitive children who hunt not just as a means of survival but for the pleasure of killing.

In "Thirst and the Boy" a meaningful exchange takes place between the boy and a bird whose gray feathers denote age and the color the boy himself will turn as he dies from lack of water (Matute 67-68). The sudden removal of the water source indicates the arbitrary way of doing things in Franco's Spain. There is no explanation for why it was so abruptly cut off and the boy searches for the water in *"el caño oxidado de la fuente, que le miraba con su único ojo ciego, muy triste"* (Matute 67) (the fountain's rusted pipe, which looked very sadly back at him with its single, sightless eye). Comparing the opening of the rusted pipe to a blind eye reinforces the circumstances in which lack of political insight and partisan justice led to systematic deprivation for many as the dictator's blatant triumphalism brought about the disintegration of Spain (Romero Salvadó 125). The absence of water suggests the drying up of the future and possibilities for countless young Spaniards. The child refuses to drink from any other water source implying that he will not drink from waters sullied by injustice. Thus he turns pale from dehydration and eventually becomes *"un montoncito de sed. El viento lo esparció, lejos"* (Matute 68) (a little pile of thirst. The wind scattered him far and wide). Then, *"llegaron los hombres y arrancaron el pilón de la fuente"* (Matute 68) (men came and wrenched out the fountain's basin). This latter detail represents the desire by the Franco regime to change the historical past to create a more pleasing picture of events (Romero Salvadó 128). The birds with the black eyes who hide among the branches of the trees signify evil ever lurking (Matute 69). The boy's spirit returns by means of the water that now flows freely and no one can quiet his haunting voice (Matute 69). Implicit is the promise to spread the truth of what happened during the Franco years and never to forget.

"The Boy Whose Friend Died" opens with a fence as the symbolic dividing line between life and death. There is the actual physical death of the friend and also the loss of the protagonist's own childhood, replaced by insensitive maturity (Matute 73). After the young protagonist returns following a fruitless search for his friend, his mother informs him: *"El amigo se murió. Niño, no pienses más en él y busca otros para jugar"* (Matute 73) (Your friend died. Child, don't think about him anymore and look for other friends to play with). The mother's heartless attitude represents the apathetic mentality of the adult world. When night arrives *"con una estrella muy grande"* (Matute 73) (with a very big star), instead of staying home for supper the boy *"se fue en busca del amigo, con las canicas, el camión, la pistola de hojalata y el reloj que no andaba"* (Matute 74) (left and went in search of his friend, bringing the marbles, the truck, the tin pistol, and the watch that didn't work). The astral light stands for the loyalty of this childhood friendship. It is interesting how the toys mentioned include items that belong to the realm of adulthood such as the pistol and the stopped watch which foreshadows the end of the protagonist's childhood too. All night the boy searches for his friend and *"fue una larga noche casi blanca, que le llenó de polvo el traje y los zapatos"* (Matute 74) (it was a long night, almost white, that made his clothes and shoes dusty). The whiteness of this long night prefigures both initiation and the emotional emptiness that attends adulthood in this society. The passage of psychological time is marked by the dust on the boy's clothing and shoes as the boy emerges from the darkness into the light of morning a more mature, colder version of himself. The hole into which the protagonist tosses the toys represents the nothingness to which he now relegates memories of his friend (Matute 74). The child he was is now buried also and he has become someone far less interesting and quixotic. Nobility of spirit has been replaced by a desire merely to fill his stomach (Matute 74). Approvingly it seems, the mother notices that the boy has grown in the night (Matute 74) but the reader realizes how much the boy has truly lost in abandoning the child within.

The deeply moving story "The Hunchback" describes a little hunchback who wishes to flee from the shadows where *"su padre lo escondía"* (Matute 77) (his father hid him). He yearns for his father to dress him in *"una capa roja con cascabeles encima de la corcova, y sacarlo a la boca del teatrito"* (Matute 77) (a red cape with little bells on his hump, and take him to the entrance of the little theater). The crimson of the child's cape symbolizes the red of liberal Spain. The hump is the visible representation of the lack of balance between Left and Right in a Spain deformed by a one-sided dictator who keeps the country strategically isolated from the rest of the world. Additionally, red is only one color of the Spanish flag emphasizing the lack of symmetry in Franco's Spain. Behind the scenes, the dictator is the invisible puppet master, while the father in the story stands for the Spanish people forced to maintain a façade of normalcy for fear of repercussions. Contained in the word *"jorobado"* (hunchback) is *"robado"* (robbed) and one cannot help but be reminded of how so many Spaniards were unable to participate in the flow of life because of former political affiliations that distorted them as citizens in the eyes of the dictator. Franco pulled the strings of fear declaring in 1949, "I will not give Spain any freedom in the next ten years. Then I will open my hand somewhat" (Preston 592).

As Darío Hermández affirms about "The Clay-Oven Boy," it is impossible to ignore *"el trasfondo cainita del relato, pues uno de los principales ejes temáticos del conjunto de la producción literaria de Matute es precisamente este: el conflicto entre semejantes por motivos pasionales o ideológicos"* (301) (the Cain-like background of the story because one of the principal thematic focal points in all of Matute's literary works is precisely this: the conflict between equals due to passionate or ideological motives). The connection to the biblical story is emphasized with the garden setting for the sinful deed (Matute 79-80). The shadows in the garden accentuate both the darkness of the act and the young boy's actual ignorance as to the significance of what he is doing. Moreover, the darkness of night foreshadows the deep sadness his parents will feel in the cold light of day at the loss of their little baby and their older child who will be replaced in their eyes by a monster. What makes this a brilliant piece of storytelling is that the reader feels almost as sorry for the *"niño de los hornos"* (Matute 79) (clay-oven boy) as for the *"conejillo despellejado"* (Matute 79) (little skinned rabbit). Incited by jealousy and loneliness, the boy seeks a solution to remove the rival of his parents' affection. Although what he does is ostensibly malevolent, Matute reveals the simple understanding that overlays the boy's actions. A civil war in miniature, there are victims on all sides. The matter-of-factness of the narration and lack of coloristic details other than light and dark imagery heighten the horror.

The first three lines of "Sea" enclose considerable symbolism: *"Pobre niño. Tenía las orejas muy grandes, y cuando se ponía de espaldas a la ventana, se volvían encarnadas. Pobre niño, estaba doblado, amarillo"* (Matute 81) (Poor child. He had very big ears and, when he stood with his back to the window, they turned red. Poor child, he was doubled over, yellow). His back to the window, this child has turned away from the sunlight gushing in the window and from life. Incidental or not, the colors of the ailing boy are those of the Spanish flag. The doctor recommends the sea as a cure; the boy imagines the sea in womb-like terms: *"El niño se figuró que el mar era como estar dentro de una caracola grandísima, llena de rumores, cánticos, voces que gritaban muy lejos, con un largo eco. Creía que el mar era alto y verde"* (Matute 81) (The boy imagined the sea was like being inside a huge conch shell, full of murmurings, songs, voices that cried from afar, followed by a long echo. He imagined the sea as being tall and green). The color green, associated with peace and tranquility, is what the boy truly desires.

The frothy whiteness of the waves produces a sense of sadness because this child will never grow old and white-haired. Even the boy's mother to whom he had announced his intention to see how high the water could climb up his body does not attempt to stop him: *"El mar, ¡qué cosa rara!, crecía, se volvía azul, violeta. Le llegó a las rodillas. Luego, a la cintura, al pecho, a los labios, a los ojos. Entonces, le entró en las orejas el eco largo, las voces que llaman lejos. Y en los ojos, todo el color"* (Matute 82) (The sea, what a strange thing!, it swelled, turned blue, violet. It reached to his knees. Then, to his waist, his chest, his lips, his eyes. Then in his ears he heard the long echo, the voices that cry from afar. And in his eyes, a burst of all colors). The blue and violet portend the coldness of the boy who has found everlasting solace and peace in the green sea. In a broader context, the emphasis on ears and hearing in this story implies how adults may have sickened the boy with their ideologies. Ultimately the child rejects the world of adults because *"no entendían nada de nada"* (Matute 82) (they didn't understand anything at all). Matute thus shows how the children of Franco's Spain are unwell; the future is disappearing while adults merely stand on the sidelines, watching helplessly.

In the first story of *The Foolish Children* a girl escapes from her sad life into the warm embrace of the welcoming earth. A sickly boy in the final narrative finds serenity and freedom from pain in the watery womb of the sea. The willing death of so many of Ana María Matute's young protagonists, who live in a world where animals are kinder than humans, is a severe indictment against society. In these brief, unforgettable stories, colors acquire many shades of meaning. With the discerning eye of an artist, Ana María Matute employs bright, bold tones or sometimes soft, impressionistic tints to express her profound pessimism with the Spain that Franco ruled. Possibly she hoped her stories would serve as a catalyst for change.

A Brief Note on This Translation

Translators of Ana María Matute's works find themselves conscientiously (and impossibly) trying to capture that intangible fairy dust that shimmers throughout her poetic prose. Acknowledging this challenge, we remained faithful to Ana María Matute's intentions as we understood them when we made subtle changes regarding syntax, word choices, and punctuation to retain her lyricism and general tone. We preferred to call attention to her artistry (as best we could) over a consistently literal translation that would have obscured her powerful, flowing style and, at times, would even have rendered her writing dissonant and disjointed to English readers. During the translation drafting process, we carefully considered Ana María Matute's collection both as a work of art in itself, inspiring eternal emotions and reflections, as well as a creation belonging to a specific cultural and historical context.

Certainly there is no substitute for reading a work in its original language and yet for so many texts that deserve a wider audience for numerous reasons, translation becomes the golden key.

We were a merry team as a mother and daughter working together. María del Carmen Luengo Santaló was born and raised in Franco's Spain while daughter Aileen Dever was born and grew up in the United States. María del Carmen Luengo Santaló holds a master's degree in Spanish from Central Connecticut State University and has taught both high school and college for many years. Aileen Dever has a Ph.D. in Spanish from the University of Connecticut and is a Professor of Spanish in the Modern Languages Department at Quinnipiac University, CT.

The micro-fiction stories reprinted and translated here with permission from *Agencia Literaria Carmen Balcells, S.A.* come from *Los niños tontos* published in Barcelona by *Destino* in 1980.

WORKS CITED

Abellán, Manuel L. *Censura y creación literaria en España (1939-1976)*. Barcelona: Ediciones Península, 1980.

Andrés-Suárez, Irene. "Formas mixtas del microrrelato." *Narrativas de la posmodernidad del cuento al microrrelato*. Ed. Salvador Montesa. Málaga: Aedile, 2009. 21-48.

Barrettini, Celia. "Ana María Matute, La Novelista Pintora." *Cuadernos hispanoamericanos* 48 (1961): 405-412.

Calafell Sala, Núria. "La conjura de la invisibilidad: El sujeto infantil en algunos cuentos de Ana María Matute y Silvina Ocampo." *Lectora* 16 (2010): 161-176.

Díaz, Janet. *Ana María Matute*. New York: Twayne, 1971.

García Lorca, Federico. "Romance de la luna, luna." *Collected Poems*. Ed. Christopher Maurer. New York: Farrar, Straus and Giroux, 2002.

Gazarian Gautier, Marie-Lise. *Interviews with Spanish Writers*. Elmwood Park, IL: Dalkey Archive P., 1991.

Gómez de Silva, Guido. *Elsevier's Concise Spanish Etymological Dictionary*. New York: Elsevier Science Pub., 1985.

Harper, Sandra N. *Puntos de vista: Narrativa moderna española*. Lexington, Massachusetts: D.C. Heath, 1993.

Hernández, Darío. "El microrrelato en los años cincuenta. Una autora española: Ana María Matute." *Narrativas de la posmodernidad del cuento al microrrelato*. Ed. Salvador Montesa. Málaga: Aedile, 2009. 297-312.

Lagmanovich, David. *El microrrelato, teoría e historia*. Palencia: Menoscuarto, 2006.

López Guil, Itzíar. "Los niños tontos de Ana María Matute: La brevedad como estrategia de manipulación discursiva." *La era de la brevedad. El microrrelato hispánico*. Eds. Irene Andrés-Suárez and Antonio Rivas. Palencia: Menoscuarto, 2008. 331-345.

Matute, Ana María. *Los niños tontos*. Barcelona: Destino, 1980.

Moix, Ana María. "La 'akadémika' con ojos de niña." *La Palabra Mágica de Ana María Matute Premio Cervantes 2010*. Ministerio de Cultura. Alcalá: U de Alcalá, 2011.

Mora, Rosa. "Escribo para ser libre." 2001. *La Palabra Mágica de Ana María Matute Premio Cervantes 2010*. Ministerio de Cultura. Alcalá: U de Alcalá, 2011.

Navarro Romero, Rosa María. "El microrrelato: género literario del siglo XXI." *Narrativas de la posmodernidad del cuento al microrrelato.* Ed. Salvador Montesa. Málaga: Aedile, 2009. 443-456.

Nextext. *Ana María Matute.* Evanston, Illinois: McDougal Littell, 2001.

Nichols, Geraldine. *Escribir, Espacio Propio: Laforet, Matute, Moix, Tusquets, Riera y Roig por Si Mismas.* Minneapolis: Institute for the Study of Ideologies and Literature, 1989.

Ortuño Ortín, María Paz. "El arzadú o la imaginación: Ana María Matute en su universo." *La Palabra Mágica de Ana María Matute Premio Cervantes 2010.* Ministerio de Cultura. Alcalá: U de Alcalá, 2011.

Pérez, Janet. "The Fictional World of Ana María Matute: Solitude, Injustice, and Dreams." *Women Writers of Contemporary Spain, Exiles in the Homeland.* Ed. Joan L. Brown. Newark: U of Delaware P, 1991. 93-112.

Preston, Paul. *Franco.* New York: BasicBooks, 1994.

Redondo Goicoechea, Alicia. *Ana María Matute (1926-).* Madrid: Ediciones del Orto, 2000.

Ródenas de Moya, Domingo. "El microrrelato en la estética de la brevedad del arte nuevo." *La era de la brevedad. El microrrelato hispánico.* Eds. Irene Andrés-Suárez and Antonio Rivas. Palencia: Menoscuarto, 2008. 77-121.

Romero Salvadó, Francisco J. *Twentieth-Century Spain: Politics and Society in Spain, 1898-1998.* New York: St. Martin's P, 1999.

Schwartz, Ronald. *Spain's New Wave Novelists, 1950-1974: Studies in Spanish Realism.* Metuchen: Scarecrow, 1976.

Shua, Ana María. "Esas feroces criaturas." *La era de la brevedad. El microrrelato hispánico.* Eds. Irene Andrés-Suárez and Antonio Rivas. Palencia: Menoscuarto, 2008. 581-586.

Tremlett, Giles. *Ghosts of Spain.* New York: Walker, 2006.

Turnbull, Patrick. *The Spanish Civil War 1936-39.* London: Osprey, 1978.

Víllora, Pedro Manuel. "Yo me siento Alicia, siempre estoy atravesando el espejo." *La Palabra Mágica de Ana María Matute Premio Cervantes 2010.* Ministerio de Cultura. Alcalá: U de Alcalá, 2011.

Vronsky, Peter. *Serial Killers, The Method and Madness of Monsters.* New York: Berkley, 2004.

LOS NIÑOS TONTOS

THE FOOLISH CHILDREN

LA NIÑA FEA

La niña tenía la cara oscura y los ojos como endrinas. La niña llevaba el cabello partido en dos mechones, trenzados a cada lado de la cara. Todos los días iba a la escuela, con su cuaderno lleno de letras y la manzana brillante de la merienda. Pero las niñas de la escuela le decían: "Niña fea"; y no le daban la mano, ni se querían poner a su lado, ni en la rueda ni en la comba: "Tú vete, niña fea". La niña fea se comía su manzana, mirándolas desde lejos, desde las acacias, junto a los rosales silvestres, las abejas de oro, las hormigas malignas y la tierra caliente de sol. Allí nadie le decía: "Vete". Un día, la tierra le dijo: "Tú tienes mi color". A la niña le pusieron flores de espino en la cabeza, flores de trapo y de papel rizado en la boca, cintas azules y moradas en las muñecas. Era muy tarde, y todos dijeron: "Qué bonita es". Pero ella se fue a su color caliente, al aroma escondido, al dulce escondite donde se juega con las sombras alargadas de los árboles, flores no nacidas y semillas de girasol.

THE UGLY GIRL

The girl's face was dark and she had eyes like sloes. The girl wore her hair parted in two locks, braided on either side of her face. Every day she would go to school, with her notebook filled with writing and a shiny apple for a snack. But the schoolgirls would say to her: "Ugly girl;" and they would not hold out their hands to her or stand next to her, either when playing in a circle or jumping rope: "Go away from here, ugly girl." The ugly girl would eat her apple, watching them from far away, from the acacias, beside the wild rose bushes, the golden honeybees, the malignant ants and the sun-warmed earth. There nobody said to her: "Go away." One day, the earth whispered to her: "You have my same color." They placed hawthorn flowers on the girl's head, rag and curly paper flowers in her mouth, blue and purple ribbons on her wrists. It was very late, and everybody said: "How pretty she is." But she went to her warm color, to the hidden perfumes, to the sweet hiding place where she could play with the long shadows of the trees, with the blossoms yet to be born and the sunflower seeds.

EL NIÑO QUE ERA AMIGO DEL DEMONIO

Todo el mundo, en el colegio, en la casa, en la calle, le decía cosas crueles y feas del demonio, y él le vio en el infierno de su libro de doctrina, lleno de fuego, con cuernos y rabo ardiendo, con cara triste y solitaria, sentado en la caldera. "Pobre demonio – pensó –, es como los judíos, que todo el mundo les echa de su tierra." Y, desde entonces, todas las noches decía: "Guapo, hermoso, amigo mío" al demonio. La madre, que le oyó, se santiguó y encendió la luz: "Ah, niño tonto, ¿tú no sabes quién es el demonio?". "Sí – dijo él –, sí: el demonio tienta a los malos, a los crueles. Pero yo, como soy amigo suyo, seré bueno siempre, y me dejará ir tranquilo al cielo."

THE BOY WHO WAS FRIENDS WITH THE DEVIL

Everyone in school, at home, on the street, told him cruel and ugly things about the devil, and he himself saw in his catechism book the devil in hell, ablaze, with burning horns and tail, with a sad and lonely face, perched on his fiery cauldron. "Poor devil," he thought. "He's like the Jews, who are driven out from every land." And so, every night he said: "Handsome, good-looking, my friend" to the devil. His mother, who heard him, crossed herself and snapped on the light: "Oh, foolish boy, don't you know who the devil is?" "Yes," replied the boy. "Yes: the devil tempts bad people, cruel people. But being a friend to him, I'll always be good and he will let me go in peace to heaven."

POLVO DE CARBÓN

La niña de la carbonería tenía polvo negro en la frente, en las manos y dentro de la boca. Sacaba la lengua al trozo de espejo que colgó en el pestillo de la ventana, se miraba el paladar, y le parecía una capillita ahumada. La niña de la carbonería abría el grifo que siempre tintineaba, aunque estuviera cerrado, con una perlita tenue. El agua salía fuerte, como chascada en mil cristales contra la pila de piedra. La niña de la carbonería abría el grifo del agua los días que entraba el sol, para que el agua brillara, para que el agua se triplicase en la piedra y en el trocito de espejo. Una noche, la niña de la carbonería despertó porque oyó a la luna rozando la ventana. Saltó precipitadamente del colchón y fue a la pila, donde a menudo se reflejaban las caras negras de los carboneros. Todo el cielo y toda la tierra estaban llenos, embadurnados del polvo negro que se filtra por debajo de las puertas, por los resquicios de las ventanas, mata a los pájaros y entra en las bocas tontas que se abren como capillitas ahumadas. La niña de la carbonería miró a la luna con gran envidia. "Si yo pudiera meter las manos en la luna", pensó. "Si yo pudiera lavarme la cara con la luna, y los dientes, y los ojos." La niña abrió el grifo, y, a medida que el agua subía, la luna bajaba, bajaba, hasta chapuzarse dentro. Entonces la niña imitó. Estrechamente abrazada a la luna, la madrugada vio a la niña en el fondo de la tina.

COAL DUST

The girl in the coal store had black dust on her brow, on her hands and inside her mouth. She would stick out her tongue in the shard of mirror she'd hung from the window lock, examining her palate, and it seemed to her a smoky little chapel. The girl from the coal store turned on the water tap that always tink-tinked even when off, with a delicate pearl. The water gushed out, as if splintering into a thousand crystals against the stone washbasin. The girl from the coal store turned on the water tap on sunny days so that the water would shine, so that the water would multiply threefold on the stone and the little mirror fragment. One night, the girl from the coal store woke up because she heard the moon caressing the window. She quickly jumped up from her mattress and went to the washbasin, where the black faces of the coalmen were often reflected. The entire sky and the entire earth were covered, caked in black dust that filters under the doors, through the narrow cracks of windows, that kills birds and enters silly mouths that open like smoky little chapels. The girl from the coal store eyed the moon enviously. "If I could only sink my hands into the moon," she thought. "If I could wash my face with the moon, and my teeth, and my eyes." The girl turned on the tap, and, as the water rose in the basin, the moon came down lower, lower, until it plunged into the water. Then the girl did the same thing. Tightly hugging the moon, the dawn found the girl at the bottom of the washbasin.

EL NEGRITO DE LOS OJOS AZULES

Una noche nació un niño.

Supieron que era tonto porque no lloraba y estaba negro como el cielo. Lo dejaron en un cesto, y el gato le lamía la cara. Pero, luego, tuvo envidia y le sacó los ojos. Los ojos eran azul oscuro, con muchas cintas encarnadas. Ni siquiera entonces lloró el niño, y todos lo olvidaron.

El niño crecía poco a poco, dentro del cesto, y el gato, que le odiaba, le hacía daño. Mas él no se defendía, porque era ciego.

Un día llegó a él un viento muy dulce. Se levantó, y con los brazos extendidos y las manos abiertas, como abanicos, salió por la ventana.

Fuera, el sol ardía. El niño tonto avanzó por entre una hilera de árboles, que olían a verde mojado y dejaban sombra oscura en el suelo. Al entrar en ella, el niño se quedó quieto, como si bebiera música. Y supo que le hacían falta, mucha falta, sus dos ojos azules.

– Eran azules – dijo el niño negro –. Azules, como chocar de jarros, el silbido del tren, el frío. ¿Dónde estarán mis ojos azules? ¿Quién me devolverá mis ojos azules?

Pero tampoco lloró, y se sentó en el suelo. A esperar, a esperar.

Sonaron el tambor y la pandereta, los cascabeles, el fru-fru de las faldas amarillas y el suave rastreo de los pies descalzos. Llegaron dos gitanas, con un oso grande. Pobre oso grande, con la piel agujereada. Las gitanas vieron al niño tonto y negro. Le vieron quieto, las manos en las rodillas, las cuencas de los ojos rojas y frescas, y no

THE LITTLE BLUE-EYED BLACK BOY

One night a child was born.

They found out he was witless because he didn't cry and was black like the sky. They left him in a basket, and the cat would lick his face. But then, the cat was envious and scratched out his eyes. The eyes were dark blue, with many red ribbons. Not even then did the child cry, and everyone forgot all about him.

The child grew little by little, inside the basket, and the cat that hated him would hurt him. But he did not defend himself because he was blind.

He felt a very sweet wind one day. He raised himself up, and with arms extended and hands open fan-like, he left through the window.

Outside, the sun was burning. The foolish child walked among a row of trees, which smelled of wet greenery and cast dark shadows on the ground. As he walked into the shadows, the child stood still, as if drinking music. And he knew he was in need, in great need, of his blue eyes.

"They were blue," the black boy said. "Blue, like the chink of ceramics, like the whistle of the train, like the cold. Where can my blue eyes be? Who will return my blue eyes to me?"

But even then he didn't cry, instead he sat on the ground. To wait, to wait.

He heard the drum and the tambourine, the bells, the swish of yellow skirts and the gentle dragging of unshod feet. Two gypsy women came, with a big bear. Poor big bear with a punctured hide. The gypsies spied the foolish, black boy. They saw him motionless, hands on knees, the

le creyeron vivo. Pero el oso, al mirar su cara negra, dejó de bailar. Y se puso a gemir y llorar por él.

Las gitanas hostigaron al animal: le pegaron, y le maldijeron sus palabras de cuchillo. Hasta que sintieron en el espinazo un aliento de brujas y se alejaron, con pies de culebra. Ataron una cuerda al cuello del oso y se lo llevaron a rastras, llenas de polvo.

Cayeron todas las hojas de los árboles, y, en lugar de la sombra, bañó al niño tonto el color rojo y dorado. Los troncos se hicieron negros y muy hermosos. El sol corría carretera adelante cuando apareció, a lo lejos, un perro color canela que no tenía dueño. El niño sintió sus pasos cerca y creyó oír que le daba vueltas a la cola, como un molino. Pensó que estaba contento.

– Dime, perro sin amo, ¿viste mis dos ojos azules?

El perro se puso las patas en sus hombros y lamió su cabeza de uvas negras. Luego, lloró largamente, muy largamente. Sus ladridos se iban detrás del sol, ya escondido en el país de las montañas.

Cuando volvió el día, el niño dejó de respirar. El perro, tendido a sus pies toda la noche, derramó dos lágrimas. Tintinearon, como pequeñas campanillas. Acostumbrado a andar en la tierra, con las uñas hizo un hondo agujero que olía a lluvia y a gusanitos partidos, a mariquitas rojas punteadas de negro. Escondió al niño dentro. Bien escondido, para que nadie, ni los ocultos ríos, ni los gnomos, ni las feroces hormigas, le encontraran.

Llegó el tiempo de los aguaceros y del aroma tibio, y florecieron dos miosotis gemelos en la tierra roja del niño tonto y negro.

hollows of his eyes red and fresh, and they didn't think he was alive. But the bear, looking at his black face, stopped dancing. And began to moan and cry for him.

The gypsy women started whipping the animal: they whacked it, and they cursed at it with their cutting words. Until they felt witches' breath at their backs and left on their snake-like feet. Tying a rope around the bear's neck, they dragged it away, all covered in dust as they were.

The leaves fluttered down from the trees, and instead of dark shade, the foolish child was bathed in colors of crimson and gold. The tree trunks became black and very beautiful. The sun was running ahead on the road when a cinnamon-colored dog appeared in the distance without an owner. The child felt its steps near him and heard its tail flapping like a windmill. It seemed happy, he thought.

"Tell me dog without an owner, have you seen my two blue eyes?"

The dog placed its paws on his shoulders and licked the child's head, a riot of curls like a bunch of black grapes. Then the animal cried bitterly for a long, long time. Its barking followed the sun, already hidden in the mountainous country.

When daylight returned, the child stopped breathing. The dog, lying at the child's feet all night, shed two tears. They clinked, like little bells. Accustomed to wandering the earth, it dug with its nails a deep hole which smelled of rain and sliced worms, of red ladybugs with black dots. The dog hid the child in it. Well hidden, so that nobody, not the hidden streams, not the gnomes, not the ferocious ants would find him.

The season of heavy rains came with warm perfumes, and twin forget-me-nots bloomed in the red earth of the foolish black child.

EL AÑO QUE NO LLEGÓ

El niño debía cumplir un año. Salió a la puerta y miró el borde de las cosas, donde se puso una luz de color distinto a todo. "Voy a cumplir un año, esta noche, a las diez", dijo. La luz se hizo más viva, extendiéndose, llenando la corteza del cielo. El niño tendió los brazos y empezó a andar, torpemente. Tenía, sujeto a cada pie, un saquito de arena dorada. Oyó el grito estridente de los vencejos. Subían, como una salpicadura de tinta, hacia aquella luz hermosa. "Voy a cumplir un año, esta noche, a las diez." Pero el grito de los vencejos agujereó la corteza de luz, el color que era distinto a todas las cosas, y aquel año, nuevo, verde, tembloroso, huyó. Escapó por aquel agujero, y no se pudo cumplir.

THE YEAR THAT NEVER CAME

The child was about to be one year old. He went to the door and looked at the edge of things, where everything shone with a different kind of light. "I will be one year old tonight at ten," he said. The light became brighter, filling the outer shell of the sky. The child stretched out his arms and began to walk, clumsily. He had, tied to each foot, a little sack of golden sand. He heard the strident cries of black swifts. The birds rose, like splashes of ink, towards that beautiful light. "I will be one year old tonight at ten." But the shrill cries of the black swifts pierced the shell of light, the color that was different from all other things, and that year, new, green, trembling, fled. The child escaped through that hole, and never reached his first year.

EL INCENDIO

El niño cogió los lápices color naranja, el lápiz largo amarillo y aquél por una punta azul y la otra rojo. Fue con ellos a la esquina, y se tendió en el suelo. La esquina era blanca, a veces la mitad negra, la mitad verde. Era la esquina de la casa, y todos los sábados la encalaban. El niño tenía los ojos irritados de tanto blanco, de tanto sol cortando su mirada con filos de cuchillo. Los lápices del niño eran naranja, rojo, amarillo y azul. El niño prendió fuego a la esquina con sus colores. Sus lápices – sobre todo aquel de color amarillo, tan largo – se prendieron de los postigos y las contraventanas, verdes, y todo crujía, brillaba, se trenzaba. Se desmigó sobre su cabeza, en una hermosa lluvia de ceniza, que le abrasó.

THE FIRE

The child grabbed the orange pencil, the long yellow pencil, and the one that was blue-tipped on one end and red on the other. He took them out to the corner and lay down on the ground. The corner was white, sometimes half black, half green. It was the corner of the house, and every Saturday they whitewashed it. The child's eyes were irritated by all that whiteness, all that sun that cut into his look like the blade of a knife. The child's pencils were orange, red, yellow, and blue. The child set the corner on fire with all his colors. His pencils – especially that yellow one, so long – caught fire from the green shutters and window coverings, and everything crackled, flared, and curled. It all crumbled and splintered on his head, a spectacular shower of ash, that swallowed him up in flames.

EL HIJO DE LA LAVANDERA

Al hijo de la lavandera le tiraban piedras los niños del administrador porque iba siempre cargado con un balde lleno de ropa, detrás de la gorda que era su madre, camino de los lavaderos. Los niños del administrador silbaban cuando pasaba, y se reían mucho viendo sus piernas, que parecían dos estaquitas secas, de esas que se parten con el calor, dando un chasquido. Al niño de la lavandera daban ganas de abrirle la cabeza pelada, como un melón-cepillo, a pedradas; la cabeza alargada y gris, con costurones, la cabeza idiota, que daba tanta rabia. Al niño de la lavandera un día le bañó su madre en el barreño, y le puso jabón en la cabeza rapada, cabeza-sandía, cabeza-pedrusco, cabeza-cabezón-cabezota, que había que partírsela de una vez. Y la gorda le dio un beso en la monda lironda cabezorra, y allí donde el beso, a pedrada limpia le sacaron sangre los hijos del administrador, esperándole escondidos, detrás de las zarzamoras florecidas.

THE WASHERWOMAN'S SON

The overseer's children threw stones at the washerwoman's son because he was always laden with a tub full of clothes, following his fat mother, on her way to the wash house. The overseer's children whistled as he went by, and they laughed uproariously at his legs that resembled two dried sticks, like those that break with a snap in the heat. The overseer's children would have liked to throw stones and crack open the washerwoman's son's bald head that was like a melon-brush; that long and gray head, with large scars, the idiot head that enraged them. One day the washerwoman was bathing her son in the tub, soaping his shaved head, his watermelon-head, his rock-head, his big-big-biggety-big head, which should be cracked open once and for all. And the fat woman planted a smooch on his hairless head, and in the same spot where she kissed him, he was bloodied by a rock thrown by the overseer's children who'd been secretly lying in wait for him among the flowering brambles.

EL ÁRBOL

Todos los días, cuando volvía del colegio, el niño que soñaba miraba aquella gran ventana del palacio. Dentro de la ventana había un árbol. El niño no lo podía comprender, y ni siquiera en sueños podía explicárselo. Alguna vez le decía a su madre: "En ese palacio, dentro de la habitación, al otro lado del cristal de la ventana, tienen un árbol". La madre le miraba con ojos serios y fijos. De pronto, parecía que tenía miedo, y le ponía la mano en la cabeza: "No importa, niño", le decía. Pero el recuerdo del árbol perseguía al niño fuera de sus sueños. "Vi el árbol ayer por la mañana y ayer por la tarde, dentro de la habitación. Los de ese palacio tienen un árbol en el centro de la sala. Yo lo he visto. Es el árbol gemelo del que vive en la acera, dentro de su cuadrito de tierra, entre el cemento. Sí, madre, es el árbol gemelo, les vi ayer hacerse muecas con las ramas." Como no podía ya pensar en otra cosa, hasta sus sueños le abandonaron. Cuando llegaron los días sin mañana, sin tarde, ni noche, cuando la mano de la madre se quedaba mucho rato en su frente, para frenar su pensamiento, el niño buscaba afanosamente en el suelo de su cuartito y debajo de la cama: "Tal vez el árbol me vaya buscando por debajo de la tierra, y vaya empujando la tierra, y me encuentre". El miedo de la madre le llegaba al niño a la garganta y sus dientes castañeteaban. "No importa, niño."

Por fin, un día, vino la noche. Entró en el cuarto y se lo llevó todo. "Madre, qué árbol tan grande", dijo el niño, perdido entre sus ramas. Pero ni siquiera oía ya la voz que repetía: "No importa niño, no importa".

THE TREE

Every day, returning home from school, the dreamy-souled child looked at the big window of the palace. Inside the window was a tree. The child could not understand it, not even in his dreams could he explain it. At times he would say to his mother: "In that palace, inside the room, on the other side of the glass, they have a tree." The mother stared at him, her eyes fixed and serious. Suddenly, she looked scared, and put a hand on his head. "Don't worry, child," she said to him. But the memory of the tree dogged the child outside of his dreams. "I saw the tree yesterday morning and yesterday afternoon inside the room. The people in that palace have a tree in the middle of their living room. I have seen it. It is the twin tree of the one that lives on the sidewalk, inside its little square of earth, surrounded by cement. Yes, mother, it is the twin tree, I saw them gesturing to each other with their branches yesterday." As he couldn't think of anything else anymore, even his dreams deserted him. When the days without morning, without afternoon, without night came, when his mother's hand remained long on his brow, as if to slow his thinking, the child eagerly searched the floor of his room and under the bed: "Maybe the tree is looking for me underground and is pushing up the earth and will find me." The mother's fear reached the child and gripped his throat and his teeth chattered. "Don't worry, child."

Finally, one day, the night came. It entered the room and took everything. "Mother, what a big tree," the child said, lost among its branches. But he was no longer hearing the voice saying over and over, "Don't worry, child, don't worry."

EL NIÑO QUE ENCONTRÓ UN VIOLÍN
EN EL GRANERO

Entre los hijos del granjero había uno de largos cabellos dorados, curvándose como virutas de madera. Nadie le oyó hablar nunca, pero tenía la voz hermosa, que no decía ninguna palabra, y, sin embargo, se doblaba como un junco, se tensaba como la cuerda de un arco, caía como una piedra, a veces; y otras parecía el ulular del viento por el borde de la montaña.

A este niño le llamaban Zum-Zum. Nadie sabía por qué, como, quizás, ni la misma granjera – siempre atareada de un lado para otro, siempre con las manos ocupadas – sabía cuándo llegó el muchacho al mundo. Zum-Zum no hacía caso de nadie. Si le llamaban los niños, se alejaba, y los niños pensaban que creció demasiado para unirse a sus juegos. Si los hermanos mayores le requerían, también Zum-Zum se alejaba, y todos pensaban que aún era demasiado pequeño para el trabajo. A veces, entre sus quehaceres, la granjera levantaba la cabeza y le veía pasar, como el rumor de una hoja. Se fijaba en sus pies sin zuecos, y se decía: "Cubriré esos pies heridos. Debo cubrirlos, para que no los corte la escarcha, ni los enlode la lluvia, ni los muerdan las piedras". Pero luego Zum-Zum se alejaba, y ella olvidaba, entre tantos muchachos, a cuál debía comprar zuecos. Si se ponía a contarlos con los dedos, las cuentas salían mal al llegar a Zum-Zum: ¿entre quiénes nació?, ¿entre Pedro y Juan?, ¿entre Pablo y José? Y la granjera empezaba de nuevo sus cuentas, hasta que llegaba el olor del horno, y corría precipitadamente a la cocina.

THE CHILD WHO FOUND A VIOLIN
IN THE GRANARY

Among the farmer's children there was one with long, golden locks, curling like wood shavings. Nobody ever heard him speak, but he had a beautiful voice, saying not a word, and yet bending like a reed, tensing like a bowstring, dropping at times like a rock, and at others seeming like the wailing wind on the edge of a mountain.

They called this child Zum-Zum. Nobody knew why, not even, perhaps, the farmer's wife herself – always busy running here and there, her hands always full – knew when the child came into the world. Zum-Zum paid no attention to anybody. If the children called him, he would go away, and the children thought he had grown too old to join in their games. If the older siblings called him, Zum-Zum also went away, and they all thought he was still too young to work. Sometimes, lifting her head from her chores, the farmer's wife saw him passing by like the whisper of a leaf. She noticed his bare feet without shoes and said to herself: "I will cover those injured feet. I should cover them, so the frost doesn't cut them, nor the rain muddy them, nor the stones bite them." But then Zum-Zum would go off, and she would forget, among so many boys, which one she should buy shoes for. If she began counting them on her fingers, she always made a mistake when she got to Zum-Zum: between whom was he born? Between Pedro and Juan? Between Pablo and José? And the farmer's wife started her counting again, until she smelled the food in the oven, and would go running hurriedly into the kitchen.

Una tarde, Zum-Zum subió al granero. Fuera había llovido, pero dentro se paseaba el sol. Al borde de la ventana vio gotitas de agua, que brillaban y caían, con tintineo que le llenó de tristeza. Había también una jaula de hierro, y dentro un cuervo, atrapado por los muchachos mayores. El cuervo negro empezó a saltar, muy agitado, al verle. En una esquina dormía el perro, que levantó una oreja.

– ¡Ya está aquí! – chilló el cuervo, desesperado –. ¡Ya está aquí, para mirar y escuchar!

– Nació una tarde como ésta – dijo el perro, en cuyo lomo había muchos pelos blancos.

Zum-Zum miró en derredor con sus claros y hondos ojos, y luego empezó a buscar algo. Sabía que debía buscar algo. Había mazorcas de maíz y manzanas, pero él buscaba en los rincones oscuros. Al fin lo encontró. Y, a pesar de que su corazón se llenaba de una gran melancolía, lo tomó en sus manos. Era un viejo violín, lleno de polvo, con las cuerdas rotas.

– De nada sirve el violín, si no tiene voz – dijo el cuervo, saltando y golpeándose con los barrotes.

Zum-Zum se sentó para anudar las cuerdas, que se retorcían hurañamente.

– No te hagas daño, niño – dijo el perro –. El violín perdió su voz hace unos años, y tú apareciste en la granja, pobre niño tonto. Lo recuerdo, porque soy viejo y mi lomo está cubierto de pelos blancos.

El cuervo estaba enfadadísimo:

– ¿Para qué sirve? Es grande para jugar, es pequeño para el trabajo. Como persona, no sirve para gran cosa.

El perro bostezó, se lamió tristemente las patas y miró hacia Zum-Zum, con ojos llenos de fatalidad.

One afternoon Zum-Zum climbed up to the grain loft. Outside it had rained, but inside the sun was glowing. On the edge of the window he saw little droplets of water that shone and fell, with a tinkling that filled him with sadness. There was also an iron cage, and inside was a crow, trapped by the older boys. When it saw him, the black crow began to jump around, very agitated. The dog was sleeping in a corner and raised an ear.

"He's here now!" cawed the crow desperately. "He's here now to look and listen!"

"He was born on an afternoon like this one," said the dog, whose flank was covered with many white hairs.

Zum-Zum looked around him with his clear, deep eyes and then began to search for something. He knew he had to search for something. There were ears of corn and apples, but he was looking in the dark corners. Finally he found it. And although his heart filled with a great sadness, he took it in his hands. It was an old violin, all dusty, with broken strings.

"The violin is of no use if it has no voice," said the crow, hopping and hitting the bars.

Zum-Zum sat down to tie the strings which sullenly resisted him.

"Don't hurt yourself, boy," said the dog. "The violin lost its voice years ago, and you appeared on the farm, poor foolish child. I remember because I'm old and my flank is covered with white hairs."

The crow was furious.

"What is he good for? He's too old to play and too young to work. As a person he's not good for much."

The dog yawned, licked its paws sadly and looked at Zum-Zum with eyes foreseeing misfortune.

Zum-Zum arregló las cuerdas del violín, y bajó la escalera. El perro le siguió.

Abajo, en el patio, estaban reunidos todos los muchachos y muchachas de la granja. Al ver a Zum-Zum las muchachas dijeron:

– ¡Canta, niño tonto! Canta, que queremos escucharte.

Pero Zum-Zum no abrió los labios, de pronto cerrados, como una pequeña concha rosada y dura. Dio el violín al hermano mayor, y esperó. Miraba con ojos como pozos hondos y muy claros. El hermano mayor dijo:

– No me mires, niño tonto. Tus ojos me hacen daño.

Sentían tal deseo de oír música que, con pelos de la cola del caballo, el hermano mayor hizo un arco. También el caballo clavó en él sus ojos, negros y redondos. Y eran suplicantes, como los del niño y como los del perro. Parecían decir: "¡Oh, si no hicieras eso! Pero es preciso, es fatal, que lo hagas".

El hermano se fue de aquellos ojos, y empezó a tocar el violín. Salió una música aguda, una música terrible. Al hermano mayor le pareció que el violín se llenaba de vida, que cantaba por su propio gusto.

– ¡Es la voz de Zum-Zum, del pobre niño tonto! – dijeron las muchachas.

Todos miraron al niño tonto. Estaba en el centro del patio, con sus pequeños labios duros y rosados, totalmente cerrados. El niño levantó los brazos y cada uno de sus dedos brillaba bajo el pálido sol. Luego se curvó, se dobló de rodillas y cayó al suelo.

Corrieron todos a él, rodeándole. Le cogieron. Le tocaron la cara, los cabellos de color de paja, la boca cerrada, los pies y las manos, blandos.

Zum-Zum fixed the strings on the violin and went down the stairs. The dog followed him.

Down in the patio were all the boys and girls of the farm. Seeing Zum-Zum, the girls said to him:

"Sing, foolish boy! Sing, we want to listen to you."

But Zum-Zum didn't open his lips, clamped suddenly shut like a little seashell, rose-colored and hard. He gave the violin to the older brother and waited. He stared with eyes that resembled a clear, bottomless pit. The older brother said:

"Don't look at me, foolish boy. Your eyes hurt me."

They felt such a desire to listen to music that the older brother made a bow with hair from the horse's tail. The horse also fixed its eyes, round and black, on him. And they were entreating, like those of the boy and the dog. They seemed to say: "Oh, if only you wouldn't do that! But it is necessary, it is inevitable that you do it."

The brother looked away from the gaze of those eyes, and began to play the violin. The music was shrill, a terrible sound. The older brother felt as if the violin had come to life, that it was singing for its own amusement.

"It's the voice of Zum-Zum, of the poor foolish child!" the girls said.

They all stared at the foolish child. He was in the middle of the patio, with his small lips, rosy and hard, tightly shut. The child raised his hands, and each one of his fingers shone under the pale sun. Then he folded, went to his knees, and collapsed to the ground.

They all ran to him, surrounding him. They picked him up. They touched his face, his straw-colored hair, his closed mouth, his soft feet and hands.

En la ventana del granero, el cuervo, dentro de su jaula, aleteaba furiosamente. Pero una risa ronca le agitaba.

– ¡Oh! – dijeron todos, con desilusión –. ¡Si no era un niño! ¡Si sólo era un muñeco!

Y lo abandonaron. El perro lo cogió entre los dientes, y se lo llevó, lejos de la música y del tonto baile de la granja.

On the window of the grain loft, the crow flapped its wings furiously inside its cage. But it shook with a raspy laugh.

"Oh," they all said, disillusioned. "He wasn't a boy! He was only a doll!"

And they all left him. Between its teeth the dog picked him up, and carried him away from the music and the foolish dancing on the farm.

EL ESCAPARATE DE LA PASTELERÍA

El niño pequeño, de los pies descalzos y sucios, soñaba todas las noches que entraba dentro del escaparate. Tras el cristal había tartas de manzana, guindas rojas y salsa de caramelo, que brillaba. Aquel niño pequeño iba siempre seguido de un perro descolorido, delgado. Un perro de perfil.

Una noche, el niño se levantó con ojos extrañamente abiertos. Los ojos de aquel niño estaban barnizados de almíbar, y su boca tenía dientecillos agudos, ansiosos.

Llegó al escaparate y apoyó la frente en el cristal, que estaba frío. Sintió gran desolación en las palmas de las manos. Todo estaba apagado, y nada veía. Pero aquel niño sonámbulo volvió a su choza con las redondas pupilas, de color de miel y azúcar tostado, muy abiertas.

El sol llegó, grande, y el niño lo vio entrar. No podía cerrar los ojos y suspiraba. En aquel momento una señora caritativa asomó la cabeza por la puerta. Traía un cazo lleno de garbanzos que le habían sobrado.

– Yo no tengo hambre. Yo no tengo hambre – dijo el niño. Y la señora caritativa, escandalizada, se fue a contarlo a todo el mundo. "Yo no tengo hambre", repitió el niño, interminablemente.

El flaco perrillo se marchó de allí, con el corazón oprimido. Volvió, trayendo en la boca un trozo de escarcha, que brillaba al sol como un gran caramelo. El niño lo chupó durante toda la mañana, sin que se fundiera en su boca fría, con toda la nostalgia.

THE DISPLAY WINDOW OF THE PASTRY SHOP

The small boy, who had dirty, bare feet, dreamt every night that he was inside the pastry-shop window. Behind the glass were apple tartlets, shiny red cherries and caramel topping. A skinny, washed-out dog always followed that small child. The outline of a dog.

One night, the child got up with his eyes strangely open. The eyes of that child were coated with syrup and in his mouth were small, sharp, anxious teeth.

He arrived at the pastry-shop window and leaned his forehead against the cold glass. He felt a great desolation in the palms of his hands. Everything was dark, and he could see nothing. But that sleepwalking child returned to his shack with wide, round eyeballs, the color of honey and burnt sugar.

The sun, huge, arrived and the child watched it come in. He could not close his eyes and he sighed. At that moment a generous lady poked her head in the door. She was carrying a pot full of left-over chickpeas.

"I'm not hungry. I'm not hungry," the child said. And the generous lady, scandalized, went away to tell everyone what had happened. "I'm not hungry," the boy repeated incessantly.

The skinny little dog left with a heavy heart. It returned, carrying in its mouth a chunk of ice that shone in the sun like a huge piece of hard candy. The child sucked on it all morning long, and it didn't melt in his cold mouth, on account of all the nostalgia.

EL OTRO NIÑO

Aquel niño era un niño distinto. No se metía en el río, hasta la cintura, ni buscaba nidos, ni robaba la fruta del hombre rico y feo. Era un niño que no amaba ni martirizaba a los perros, ni los llevaba de caza con un fusil de madera. Era un niño distinto, que no perdía el cinturón, ni rompía los zapatos, ni llevaba cicatrices en las rodillas, ni se manchaba los dedos de tinta morada. Era otro niño, sin sueños de caballos, sin miedo de la noche, sin curiosidad, sin preguntas. Era otro niño, otro, que nadie vio nunca, que apareció en la escuela de la señorita Leocadia, sentado en el último pupitre, con su juboncillo de terciopelo malva, bordado en plata. Un niño que todo lo miraba con otra mirada, que no decía nada porque todo lo tenía dicho. Y cuando la señorita Leocadia le vio los dos dedos de la mano derecho unidos, sin poderse despegar, cayó de rodillas, llorando, y dijo: "¡Ay de mí, ay de mí! ¡El niño del altar estaba triste y ha venido a mi escuela!"

THE OTHER BOY

That boy was a different kind of boy. He didn't go into the river up to his waist, nor did he hunt nests, nor did he steal the fruit of the ugly rich man. He was a boy who neither loved nor tormented dogs, nor did he take them with him to hunt with a wooden rifle. He was a different kind of boy, who didn't lose his belt, who didn't break his shoes, who didn't have scars on his knees or purple ink stains on his fingers. He was another kind of boy, without dreams of horses, without fear of the night, without curiosity, without questions. He was a different kind of boy, different, never seen before, who appeared in Miss Leocadia's school, seated at the last desk, with his vest of purple velvet, embroidered in silver. A child who looked at everything with a different kind of look, who said nothing because he had said everything. And when Miss Leocadia saw the two fingers of his right hand stuck together, which could not be pulled apart, she fell to her knees crying, and said, "Oh my, oh my! The child on the altar was lonely and he has come to my school!"

LA NIÑA QUE NO ESTABA EN NINGUNA PARTE

Dentro del armario olía a alcanfor, a flores aplastadas, como ceniza en laminillas. A ropa blanca y fría de invierno. Dentro del armario una caja guardaba zapatitos rojos, con borla, de una niña. Al lado, entre papel de seda y naftalina, estaba la muñeca, grandota, con mofletes abultados y duros, que no se podían besar. En los ojos redondos, fijos, de vidrio azul, se reflejaba la lámpara, el techo, la tapa de la caja y, en otro tiempo, las copas de los árboles del parque. La muñeca, los zapatos, eran de la niña. Pero en aquella habitación no se la veía. No estaba en el espejo, sobre la cómoda. Ni en la cara amarilla y arrugada, que se miraba la lengua y se ponía bigudíes en la cabeza. La niña de aquella habitación no había muerto, mas no estaba en ninguna parte.

THE GIRL WHO WAS NOWHERE

Inside the closet it smelled of camphor, of crushed flowers, like sheets of ashes. Of cold, white, winter clothing. Inside the closet a box held little red shoes with tassels that had belonged to a little girl. Next to them, between tissue paper and mothballs, rested the doll, biggish, with hard, chubby cheeks that couldn't be kissed. Her round, staring eyes of blue glass reflected the light of the lamp, the ceiling, the lid of the box, and, in another time, treetops in the park. The doll, the shoes, all belonged to the girl. But she was nowhere to be seen in that room. She was not in the mirror above the chest of drawers. Nor could she be found in that yellowed, wrinkled face, examining her tongue and putting curlers in her hair. The girl whose room that was had not died, but she was nowhere to be seen.

EL TIOVIVO

El niño que no tenía perras gordas merodeaba por la feria con las manos en los bolsillos, buscando por el suelo. El niño que no tenía perras gordas no quería mirar al tiro al blanco, ni a la noria, ni, sobre todo, al tiovivo de los caballos amarillos, encarnados y verdes, ensartados en barras de oro. El niño que no tenía perras gordas, cuando miraba con el rabillo del ojo, decía: "Eso es una tontería que no lleva a ninguna parte. Sólo da vueltas y vueltas, y no lleva a ninguna parte". Un día de lluvia, el niño encontró en el suelo una chapa redonda de hojalata; la mejor chapa de la mejor botella de cerveza que viera nunca. La chapa brillaba tanto que el niño la cogió y se fue corriendo al tiovio, para comprar todas las vueltas. Y aunque llovía y el tiovivo estaba tapado con la lona, en silencio y quieto, subió en un caballo de oro, que tenía grandes alas. Y el tiovivo empezó a dar vueltas, vueltas, y la música se puso a dar gritos por entre la gente, como él no vio nunca. Pero aquel tiovivo era tan grande, tan grande, que nunca terminaba su vuelta, y los rostros de la feria, y los tolditos, y la lluvia, se alejaron de él. "Que hermoso es no ir a ninguna parte", pensó el niño, que nunca estuvo tan alegre. Cuando el sol secó la tierra mojada, y el hombre levantó la lona, todo el mundo huyó, gritando. Y ningún niño quiso volver a montar en aquel tiovivo.

THE CAROUSEL

The child without any change roamed around the funfair with his hands in his pockets, searching the ground. The child without any change did not want to look at the target shooting, nor at the Ferris wheel, and above all not at the carousel with its yellow, red and green horses, pierced by golden poles. When the child without any change looked out the corner of his eye, he said, "That's a foolish thing that goes nowhere. It only spins and spins and goes nowhere." One rainy day, the child found a small, round piece of tin on the ground, the best cap of the best beer bottle he had ever seen. The cap shone so much that he grabbed it and ran to the carousel to buy all the rides. And although it was raining and the carousel was covered with a tarpaulin, silently and stealthily, he mounted a golden horse with great wings. And the carousel began to go round and round, and the music began to shriek among the people, in a way he had never seen before. But that carousel was so big, so big that it never finished its spin, and the faces at the funfair, and the awnings, and the rain, went away from him. "How wonderful it is to go nowhere," thought the child who had never been so happy. When the sun dried the wet earth, and the man lifted the tarpaulin, everybody fled screaming. And no other child ever wanted to ride that carousel ever again.

EL NIÑO QUE NO SABÍA JUGAR

Había un niño que no sabía jugar. La madre le miraba desde la ventana ir y venir por los caminillos de tierra, con las manos quietas, como caídas a los dos lados del cuerpo. Al niño, los juguetes de colores chillones, la pelota, tan redonda, y los camiones, con sus ruedecillas, no le gustaban. Los miraba, los tocaba, y luego se iba al jardín, a la tierra sin techo, con sus manitas pálidas y no muy limpias, pendientes junto al cuerpo como dos extrañas campanillas mudas. La madre miraba inquieta al niño, que iba y venía con una sombra entre los ojos. "Si al niño le gustara jugar yo no tendría frío mirándole ir y venir." Pero el padre decía, con alegría: "No sabe jugar, no es un niño corriente. Es un niño que piensa".

Un día la madre se abrigó y siguió al niño, bajo la lluvia, escondiéndose entre los árboles. Cuando el niño llegó al borde del estanque, se agachó, buscó grillitos, gusanos, crías de rana y lombrices. Iba metiéndolos en una caja. Luego, se sentó en el suelo, y uno a uno los sacaba. Con sus uñitas sucias, casi negras, hacía un leve ruidito, ¡crac!, y les segaba la cabeza.

THE BOY WHO DIDN'T KNOW HOW TO PLAY

There was a boy who didn't know how to play. His mother would watch him from the window as he walked back and forth on little sandy pathways, his hands motionless, dangling on both sides of his body. The boy did not like loud-colored toys, the ball, so round, and the trucks with their itsy-bitsy wheels. He looked at the toys, he touched them, and then went to the garden, to the space without a roof, with his small hands, pale and not too clean, dangling at his sides like two strange, mute little bells. The mother anxiously watched the boy come and go with a shadow between her eyes. "If the boy liked to play, I wouldn't feel the shivers watching him come and go." But the father said joyfully: "He doesn't know how to play, he's not an ordinary boy. He's a child who ponders things."

One day the mother bundled herself up and followed the boy, in the rain, hiding among the trees. When the child reached the edge of the pond, he squatted down, looking for little crickets, caterpillars, tadpoles and earthworms. He put them in a box. Then he sat down on the ground and took them out one by one. With his little dirty nails, almost black, he made a slight sound, crack!, and sliced off their heads.

EL CORDERITO PASCUAL

Al hijo del ropavejero le regalaron un corderito pascual, para jugar con él. El hijo del ropavejero era un niño muy gordo, que no tenía amigos. Los niños del albañil, los del contable, los del zapatero, se reían de su barriga, de sus mofletes, de su repapada; y le llamaban gorrino, barril de cerveza, puerco de San Martín. El corderito pascual, en cambio, era blanco y dulce, y le pusieron un lazo verde al cuello. El hijo gordo del usurero, ropavejero, compra-venta, salía a pasear junto a la tapia soleada, en busca de las hierbecillas del solar, llevando tras sí a su amigo corderillo, que tenía una mirada como no vio nunca a nadie el hijo del ropavejero. Llegaron los días de las golondrinas, de los nidos en el tejado, de la hierbecilla tierna, de los niños que venían a dejarse el abrigo a la tienda del ropavejero. De niños que, al quitarse el abrigo, se quedaban muy estrechos, muy delgados, en sus chalecos de punto, con las mangas cortas, con las muñecas desnudas. De niños que se iban luego a la plaza, junto al capazo de la madre, con los dos duros de la compra, llorando un poco porque no había llegado el sol del todo. Llegaron los días con niños de la mano, medio a rastras, con niños despojados, de ojos redondos, con niños de dos duros, de siete pesetas, de "esto no vale nada". Los abriguitos y los pantalones de lana se amontonaban en las estanterías, junto a la naftalina, junto a las palabras de "esto no vale nada", "esto tiene una mancha", "esto está roto". El niño gordo del ropavejero besaba las orejillas del cordero pascual, del amigo que

THE LITTLE PASCHAL LAMB

The old clothes dealer's son was given a little paschal lamb to play with. The old clothes dealer's son was a very fat boy who had no friends. The bricklayer's children, the accountant's children, the shoemaker's children laughed at his belly, his chubby cheeks, his double chin, and they called him pig, beer barrel, St. Martin's hog. The paschal lamb, however, was white and sweet, and they put a green ribbon around its neck. The fat son of the moneylender, old clothes dealer, buyer and seller, walked along the sunny wall of the yard, searching for grass, pulling behind him his friend the little lamb, whose eyes had an expression that the old clothes dealer's son had never seen before. The days arrived when swallows return, days of nests on rooftops, days of tender grasses, and days when children would come to leave their coats in the store of the old clothes dealer. Children who, when they took off their coats, looked so small and skinny in their knitted vests, with short sleeves, their wrists showing. Children who would then go to the town square, beside their mother's basket, with the ten pesetas' worth of the sale, crying a little because the sun wasn't fully shining yet. The days came when children were dragged by the hand, stripped of some of their clothes, round-eyed children with two five-peseta coins, with seven pesetas, with "this is worthless." The little coats and the woolen pants were heaped onto the shelves, along with the mothballs, along with words like "this is worthless," "this has a stain," "this is ripped." The old clothes dealer's fat son kissed the little ears of his

no le llamaba cerdo, cebón, barril de cerveza. Y el día de Pascua, cuando el niño del ropavejero se sentó a la mesa llena de cuchillos y de sol sobre el mantel, vio de pronto los dientes de papá, los grandes y blancos dientes de papá-ropavejero, papá-compra-venta-no-vale-nada-prestamista-siete-pesetas-está-roto. Y el niño gordo saltó de la silla, corrió a la cocina con el corazón en la boca y vio, sobre una mesa, despellejada, la cabeza de su amigo. Mirándole, por última vez, con aquella mirada que no vio nunca en nadie.

paschal lamb, of the friend who didn't call him pig, porker, beer barrel. And on Easter Sunday, when the old clothes dealer's child sat at the table full of knives and sunshine beaming on the tablecloth, he suddenly saw papá's teeth, the big and white teeth of papá-old-clothes-dealer, papá-buyer-and-seller-it's-worthless-moneylender-seven-pesetas-it's-ripped. And the fat child leaped from his chair, ran to the kitchen, with his heart in his mouth, and saw, on top of a table, skinned, the head of his friend. Looking at him, for the last time, with that expression that he had never seen on anyone else before.

EL NIÑO DEL CAZADOR

El niño del cazador iba todos los días a la montaña, detrás de su padre, con el zurrón y el pan. A la noche volvían, con cinturones de palomas y liebres, con las piernas salpicadas de gotitas rojas, que, poco a poco, se volvían negras. El niño del cazador esperaba en el chozo de ramas, oía los tiros y los contaba en voz baja. A la noche, tropezando con las piedras, sentía los picos de las palomas, de las perdices y las codornices, de los tordos, martilleando sus rodillas. El niño del cazador soñaba hasta el alba en cacerías con escopetas y con perros. Una noche de gran luna, el niño del cazador robó la escopeta y se fue en busca de los árboles, camino arriba. El niño cazó todas las estrellas de la noche, las alondras blancas, las liebres azules, las palomas verdes, las hojas doradas y el viento puntiagudo. Cazó el miedo, el frío, la oscuridad. Cuando le bajaron, en la aurora, la madre vio que el rocío de la madrugada, vuelto rojo como vino, salpicaba las rodillas blancas del tonto niño cazador.

THE HUNTER'S BOY

The hunter's boy would go to the mountain every day, following his father, carrying the leather bag and bread. At night they returned, with pigeons and hares on their belts, their legs spattered with little red droplets which, little by little, turned black. The hunter's boy waited in the hut made of tree branches, counting in a low voice the shots he heard. At night, stumbling over stones, he felt the beaks of the pigeons, of the partridges and quails, of the thrushes, hammering into his knees. The hunter's boy dreamed until dawn of hunting with shotguns and dogs. One night when a full moon was glowing, the hunter's boy stole the shotgun and climbed up hill in search of the forest. The boy hunted all the stars of the night, the white larks, the blue hares, the green pigeons, the golden leaves and the sharp wind. He hunted fear, cold, darkness. At dawn, when they carried him down, the mother saw how the early morning dew, which had turned red as wine, was spattered on the white knees of the foolish hunter boy.

LA SED Y EL NIÑO

El niño que tenía sed iba todas las tardes, con su pan y su chocolate, hasta la fuentecita redonda del surtidor. Alrededor de la fuente la tierra olía húmeda, con huellas de pájaro. El niño que tenía sed abría la boca sobre el surtidor y el agua le cosquilleaba el paladar. Le borraba el chocolate, el pan, y la hora de la merienda.

Una tarde, el niño que tenía sed no encontró agua. Empezó a buscar y rebuscar en el caño oxidado de la fuente, que le miraba con su único ojo ciego, muy triste. En torno, la tierra estaba seca, como el paladar del niño, y los pájaros piaban dando saltos, llenos de irritación. – ¿Qué se hizo del surtidor? – preguntó el niño, con ojos severos. – Se lo llevaron los hombres – dijo el pájaro gris, el más áspero. – Lo condujeron a otro lado, y nunca, nunca volverá.

El niño que tenía sed fue todas las tardes con su paladar seco, lleno de polvo, a mirar el ojo vacío de la fuente. Poco a poco, el niño palidecía. No bebía agua. "Este niño tonto, se morirá de sed", decían los hombres, las mujeres. Los perros le miraban con ojos llenos de antigüedad y ladraban largamente: "Este niño tonto, se morirá de sed". En cambio, los pájaros no parecían tener motivo alguno de tristeza. Todas las tardes le rodeaban, nerviosos, con ojos redondos y brillantes de alegría salvaje.

El niño se volvió ceniza. Sólo era un montoncito de sed. El viento lo esparció, lejos. ¡Quién sabe adónde lo llevaría!

THIRST AND THE BOY

The thirsty boy went every afternoon, with his bread and chocolate, to the round little jetting fountain. Around the fountain there was the smell of wet earth covered with bird tracks. The thirsty boy opened his mouth over the spout and the water tickled his palate. He forgot the chocolate, bread, and the time of his afternoon snack.

One afternoon, the thirsty child found no water. He started searching and searching the fountain's rusted pipe, which looked very sadly back at him with its single, sightless eye. All around, the earth was dry like the boy's palate and the birds twittered and jumped, irritated. "What happened to the fountain spout?" asked the boy severely. "The men took it," the gray bird said, who was the harshest. "They took it somewhere else and it will never, never be returned."

The thirsty child came back every afternoon with his palate dry and dusty, to look at the empty eye of the fountain. Gradually, the boy grew pale. He wasn't drinking water. "This foolish child will die of thirst," said the men and the women. The dogs looked at him with their old eyes and barked for a long time: "This foolish boy will die of thirst." However, the birds did not seem sad at all. Every afternoon they encircled the boy, nervous, with their round eyes shining with savage glee.

The child turned to ashes. He was just a little pile of thirst. The wind scattered him far and wide. Who knows where it took him!

Después, llegaron los hombres y arrancaron el pilón de la fuente. Los pájaros, como un presagio, se escondieron en las ramas de los árboles.

Al día siguiente, el agua brotó del suelo, furiosa, en surtidor muy alto. Ocultos entre las ramas y las hojas, los pájaros movían a uno y otro lado sus negras pupilas. Oyeron la voz del niño tonto. Decía, con grande, con dulce y solemne severidad:

– ¿Quién se llevó el pilón de la fuente, la boca sedienta y vacía de mi fuente?

Nadie pudo acallar su voz. El gran surtidor bajó al suelo, alargándose, sin que nadie pudiera detenerlo. La voz del niño tonto que tenía sed bajaba, bajaba todas las tardes, todos los días. Abríase paso, entre árboles y niños que comen pan y chocolate, a las seis y media; a través de la reseca tierra, como un gran paladar, hasta el océano.

Later, men came and wrenched out the fountain's basin. The birds, like an omen, hid themselves among the branches of the trees.

The next day, the water gushed furiously from the earth, in a tall stream. Hidden among the branches and leaves, the birds' black pupils darted everywhere. They heard the foolish boy's voice. It said with great, sweet, and solemn severity:

"Who took the basin, the thirsty empty mouth of my fountain?"

No one could quiet his voice. The tall stream came down to the ground, expanding, and no one could stop it. The voice of the foolish, thirsty boy came down, came down every afternoon, every day. It made its way, among the trees and among the children who eat bread and chocolate at six-thirty, through the parched earth, like a huge palate, until it reached the ocean.

EL NIÑO AL QUE SE LE MURIÓ EL AMIGO

Una mañana se levantó y fue a buscar al amigo, al otro lado de la valla. Pero el amigo no estaba, y, cuando volvió, le dijo la madre: "El amigo se murió. Niño, no pienses más en él y busca otros para jugar." El niño se sentó en el quicio de la puerta, con la cara entre las manos y los codos en las rodillas. "Él volverá", pensó. Porque no podía ser que allí estuviesen las canicas, el camión y la pistola de hojalata, y el reloj aquel que ya no andaba, y el amigo no viniese a buscarlos. Vino la noche, con una estrella muy grande, y el niño no quería entrar a cenar. "Entra, niño, que llega el frío", dijo la madre. Pero, en lugar de entrar, el niño se levantó del quicio y se fue en busca del amigo, con las canicas, el camión, la pistola de hojalata y el reloj que no andaba. Al llegar a la cerca, la voz del amigo no le llamó, ni le oyó en el árbol, ni en el pozo. Pasó buscándole toda la noche. Y fue una larga noche casi blanca, que le llenó de polvo el traje y los zapatos. Cuando llegó el sol, el niño, que tenía sueño y sed, estiró los brazos, y pensó: "Qué tontos y pequeños son esos juguetes. Y ese reloj que no anda, no sirve para nada". Lo tiró todo al pozo, y volvió a la casa, con mucha hambre. La madre le abrió la puerta, y dijo: "Cuánto ha crecido este niño, Dios mío, cuánto ha crecido". Y le compró un traje de hombre, porque el que llevaba le venía muy corto.

THE BOY WHOSE FRIEND DIED

One morning he got up and went to look for his friend, on the other side of the fence. But his friend wasn't there, and, when he returned home, his mother told him: "Your friend died. Child, don't think about him anymore and look for other friends to play with." The boy sat on the threshold of the door, with his face in his hands and his elbows on his knees. "He will return," he thought. Because it just couldn't be that the marbles, the truck, the tin pistol, and that watch that didn't work anymore were all there, and his friend hadn't come around looking for them. Night came, with a very big star, and the boy didn't want to come in for supper. "Come in, child, it's getting cold," said his mother. But instead of coming in, the boy left and went in search of his friend, bringing the marbles, the truck, the tin pistol, and the watch that didn't work. When he got to the fence, his friend's voice didn't call to him, nor did he hear his voice in the tree or the well. He spent the whole night searching for him. And it was a long night, almost white, that made his clothes and shoes dusty. When the sun rose, the boy, who was sleepy and thirsty, stretched out his arms and thought: "How silly and small those toys are. And that watch that doesn't work isn't good for anything." He tossed everything down the well and returned home, very hungry. His mother opened the door and said: "How tall this child has grown. My God, how tall." And she bought him a man's suit because the one he had on was too small for him.

EL JOROBADO

El niño del guignol estaba siempre muy triste. Su padre tenía muchas voces, muchos porrazos, muchos gritos distintos, pero el niño estaba triste, con su joroba a cuestas, porque su padre lo escondía dentro de la lona y le traía juguetes y comida cara, en lugar de ponerle una capa roja con cascabeles encima de la corcova, y sacarlo a la boca del teatrito, con una estaca, para que dijera: "¡Toma, Cristobita, toma, toma!", y que todos se risen mucho viéndole.

THE HUNCHBACK

The puppeteer's boy was always so sad. His father had many voices, many blows, many different screams, but the boy was sad, under his hump, because his father hid him inside the tent and brought him toys and expensive food, instead of putting a red cape with little bells on his hump, and taking him to the entrance of the little theater, so he could say with a stick, "Take that, Cristobita, take that and that!" and everybody could laugh uproariously watching him.

EL NIÑO DE LOS HORNOS

Al niño que hacía hornos con barro y piedras le trajeron un hermano como un conejillo despellejado. Además, lloraba.

El niño que hacía hornos vio las espaldas de todos. La espalda del padre. El padre se inclinaba sobre el nuevo y le decía ternezas. El niño de los hornos quiso tocar los ojos del hermano, tan ciegos y brillantes. Pero el padre le pegó en la mano extendida.

A la noche, cuando todos dormían, el niño se levantó con una idea fija. Fue al rincón oscuro de la huerta, cogió ramillas secas y las hacinó en su hornito de barro y piedras. Luego fue a la alcoba, vio el brazo de la madre largo y quieto sobre la sábana. Sacó de allí al hermano y se lo llevó, en silencio. Prendió su hornito querido y metió dentro al conejo despellejado.

THE CLAY-OVEN BOY

The boy who made ovens from clay and stones was presented with a brother like a little skinned rabbit. He also cried.

The child who made ovens saw everyone's back. The back of his father. His father bending over the new arrival, cooing to him. The child who made ovens tried to touch his brother's eyes, so blind and bright. But his father slapped his outstretched hand.

At night, when everyone was asleep, the boy rose with a fixed idea. He went to the dark corner of the garden, gathered dry twigs and piled them all up in his little oven made from clay and stones. Then he went into the bedroom, saw his mother's long and motionless arm on the sheet. He plucked his brother out from there and took him outside quietly. He lit his beloved little oven and thrust the skinned rabbit inside.

MAR

Pobre niño. Tenía las orejas muy grandes muy grandes, y, cuando se ponía de espaldas a la ventana, se volvían encarnadas. Pobre niño, estaba doblado, amarillo. Vino el hombre que curaba, detrás de sus gafas. "El mar – dijo –; el mar, el mar." Todo el mundo empezó a hacer maletas y a hablar del mar. Tenían una prisa muy grande. El niño se figuró que el mar era como estar dentro de una caracola grandísima, llena de rumores, cánticos, voces que gritaban muy lejos, con un largo eco. Creía que el mar era alto y verde.

Pero cuando llegó al mar se quedó parado. Su piel, ¡qué extraña era allí! – Madre – dijo, porque sentía vergüenza –, quiero ver hasta dónde me llega el mar.

Él, que creyó el mar alto y verde, lo veía blanco, como el borde de la cerveza, cosquilleándolo, frío, la punta de los pies.

– ¡Voy a ver hasta dónde me llega el mar! – Y anduvo, anduvo, anduvo. El mar, ¡qué cosa rara!, crecía, se volvía azul, violeta. Le llegó a las rodillas. Luego, a la cintura, al pecho, a los labios, a los ojos. Entonces, le entró en las orejas el eco largo, las voces que llaman lejos. Y en los ojos, todo el color. ¡Ah, sí, por fin, el mar era verdad! Era una grande, inmensa caracola. El mar, verdaderamente, era alto y verde.

Pero los de la orilla, no entendían nada de nada. Encima, se ponían a llorar a gritos, y decían: "¡Qué desgracia! ¡Señor, qué gran desgracia!"

SEA

Poor child. He had very big ears and, when he stood with his back to the window, they turned red. Poor child, he was doubled over, yellow. The man who cured people from behind his glasses came. "The sea," he said. "The sea, the sea." Everybody started packing suitcases and talking about the sea. They were in a great rush. The boy imagined the sea was like being inside a huge conch shell, full of murmurings, songs, voices that cried from afar, followed by a long echo. He imagined the sea as being tall and green.

But when he arrived at the sea, he stopped in his tracks. His skin, how strange it looked there! "Mother," he said, because he was ashamed. "I want to see how high the sea can climb up me."

He, who thought the sea was tall and green, saw it as white, like beer froth, cold, tickling him, the tips of his toes.

"I'm going to see how high the sea can climb up me!" And he walked, walked, walked. The sea, what a strange thing!, it swelled, turned blue, violet. It reached to his knees. Then, to his waist, his chest, his lips, his eyes. Then in his ears he heard the long echo, the voices that cry from afar. And in his eyes, a burst of all colors. Ah, yes, finally, the sea was real! It was a huge, immense conch shell. The sea was truly tall and green.

But those on the shore didn't understand anything at all. They even started crying loudly and moaning: "What a tragedy! God, what a horrible tragedy!"

Read more fiction in English from Small Stations Press:

Suso de Toro, TICK-TOCK

"Possibly the most impressive novel ever written in the Galician language." With these words, the eminent critic Basilio Losada describes Suso de Toro's novel *Tick-Tock* in a letter to the author. Suso de Toro is alternative in everything he does, he rearranges the boundaries, surprises the reader, does the unexpected, persons, tenses change, and what could be construed as an atheistic, chaotic novel acquires hints of religiosity. Nano, the narrator, is a man of uncertain age who has never made it in the world, but who likes to hold forth all the same, to fill notebooks with his thoughts on fishing in the Gran Sol, on controlling his libido, on inventing machines that serve no purpose. The novel centres on his experiences, and on the lives of those around him: his mother, his father and half-brother, the people who occupy the building where his mother cleans. *Tick-Tock* , a sequel to *Polaroid*, received the Spanish Critics' Prize for its unconventionality and narrative expertise, and is the author's most popular work.

ISBN 978-954-384-056-4

Miguel-Anxo Murado, ASH WEDNESDAY

In this collection of sixteen short stories by the Galician writer
Miguel-Anxo Murado, the reader is taken on a journey through the
various rites of passage that make up an individual's life, from the
months-old baby who lives in the eternal moment of Nothingness
and quickly forgets an argument with his elder brother to the
university professor who visits a colleague in Kyoto to see the
cherry blossom and before the symbols of impermanence is forced
to confront his own terminal illness. Children and adults alike
endure extreme situations, from a child who is bullied at school
to the Chinese women workers who stay up all night to prepare a
handmade suit for the morning. Sailors are rescued at sea; others
are cast adrift when their ship sinks, at the mercy of the current.
A young man is brought face to face with his late father when
surrounded by a mountain blaze; a young girl endeavors to learn
the secrets to her sister's radiant beauty. Two boys fall for the
same girl; one tries to curry favor with the members of his gang
in a story reminiscent of Isaac Babel's *Red Cavalry*, while another
searches for the strength inside. All are caught in unexpected
situations, elegantly and expertly described, and handed the task
of how to react in a book that celebrates the human spirit across
barriers of time and language.

ISBN 978-954-384-053-3

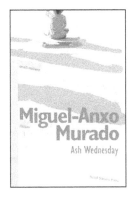

Manuel Rivas, THE POTATO EATERS

Sam is a drug addict with a sense of humour. One particular escapade lands him in hospital, where he makes friends with the old man in the adjoining bed and becomes progressively enamoured of the nurse Miss Cowbutt's unsung qualities. In an attempt to wean him off his drug habit, his elder brother, Nico, takes him to the village, Aita, where their grandmother lives, a world far removed from the distractions of modern life, in which even the silence seems animate. He meets up with Gaby the single mother and Dombodán the collector of discarded items. He also becomes acquainted with a slippery customer named "Sir" who takes refuge in the radio set in the attic. A host of colourful characters – from Tip and Top to the "relentless lady" – populate this tale, which pits a victim of zero expectations against the haunting traditions of the village.

ISBN 978-954-384-052-6

Miguel Anxo Fernández, A NICHE FOR MARILYN

Frank Soutelo is a down-at-heel private detective, the son of Galician immigrants, based in Los Angeles, California. He doesn't get much choice in his assignments and has to take pretty much what's on offer, so when he gets hired and paid an advance of twenty-five thousand dollars, he's understandably pleased, and his secretary even more so. The unusual thing, however, is what he's been asked to do: to recover the body of the actress Marilyn Monroe, which has reputedly gone missing from her grave in Westwood Village Memorial Park Cemetery. Big Frank, as he is known, is about to get drawn into a world that is unfamiliar to him: a world of necrophiliacs, zealous watchmen, uniformed chauffeurs and high-class mansions. The question is will he be able to extricate himself from this situation with his dignity and heart in one piece?

ISBN 978-954-384-051-9

Xurxo Borrazás, VICIOUS

Shakespearean drama set in a Galician context. There is something strikingly postmodern – or Elizabethan – about this novel, in which a man from Laracha, south-west of Coruña, on Galicia's famed Coast of Death, is on the run for committing a multiple murder that shocks the local community and has the priest calling for the razing of the local slums. Chucho Monteiro, who has always been overlooked by his father in favor of his younger brother, Daniel, more pliable, less violent, heads to the port of Coruña in order to effect his escape on the first ship weighing anchor, a ship that will take him not to Stratford, but to Southampton and on. In a fascinating, multi-layered narrative, the author keeps the reader guessing about the murderer's final destination until the very end. Narrative chronology is mixed up, and the veil between author and reader is torn in two, so that we're not sure if we are witnesses or partakers of this narrative. *Vicious* (called *Criminal* in Galician) is Xurxo Borrazás' second and best-known novel, and won him the Spanish Critics' Prize as well as the San Clemente Prize awarded by high-school readers.

ISBN 978-954-384-038-0

For an up-to-date list of our publications, please visit www.smallstations.com

CPSIA information can be obtained
at www.ICGtesting.com
Printed in the USA
LVHW032227171122
733429LV00003B/428

9 789543 840601